"A sapphic coming-of-age wonder that's dangerous on all sides but heartfelt to the core. Further evidence that everything Samantha Kolesnik touches turns to gold."

> — HAILEY PIPER, BRAM STOKER
> AWARD-WINNING AUTHOR
> OF *QUEEN OF TEETH*

"Otherworldly and grounded, immersive and gut-wrenching, *Elogona* feels all too real."

> — RAE KNOWLES, AUTHOR OF
> *MERCILESS WATERS*

"Apocalyptic folklore, religious fascism, and sapphic romance collide in Kolesnik's darkly magical maelstrom of a novella *Elogona*."

> — ERIC RAGLIN, AUTHOR OF
> *EXTINCTION HYMNS*

"*Elogona* enraptures immediately with darkly fantastical elements that draw you into one of the sweetest and yet devastating sapphic romances I've read. A tale of survival, from the individual to the whole of humanity as they wallow in their own messy, war-torn aftermath, it grabbed me by the throat and didn't let go until the shocking end. Layers of depth, reflecting on the state of our world, are expertly woven together by characters you can't help but fall for, all set in a future sublimely heartbreaking. Kolesnik melded genres and subverted expectations so skillfully, I know I'll be revisiting this story many times as soon as my shredded heart can bear it."

— EMMA E. MURRAY, AUTHOR OF
EXQUISITE HUNGER

"At once a dystopian fairytale and a glimpse of our too-possible future, *Elogona* is a story of love, defiance, and determination in the face of monsters—both human and inhuman. Kolesnik tears through these themes with teeth and heart, never failing to unnerve and surprise."

— J.A.W. MCCARTHY, BRAM STOKER
AWARD AND SHIRLEY JACKSON
AWARD FINALIST, AUTHOR OF *SLEEP
ALONE*

ELOGONA

Samantha Kolesnik

WEIRD
PUNK

For D,
in honor of our transcendental friendship

CONTENTS

I   1

II   45

III   97

IV   111

Acknowledgments   119

About the Author   121

Also from Weirdpunk Books   123

One person's vision for the future is another's eulogy for the past.

I

It was nearing the time of Maiden's Feast when Verna led Audrey to the beach to listen to Elogona. Audrey's parents, refugees from the mainland, didn't want their daughter spending time near the water, especially not with Verna.

The island was a mix of Eloganites, who practiced the new path, and Christians of all sects, who took their ways from the mainland to the breakaway island and tried to continue their evangelical efforts in earnest. It was the Fall of Man, they'd say, that had brought about the ecological devastation and for them, according to their Christian Bible, Elogona was a creature of Satan, brought up from the depths of Hell to punish humankind. For the Christians, Verna and "her kind" had caused the flood, the fires, and the devastation. Verna was the reason that Elogona awoke and bleated her sorrowful tune through blowholes that sounded like organ pipes.

Verna wasn't a Christian, though. She wasn't much of an Eloganite either, even though in many ways their beliefs were far more tolerable. Verna loved to worship the present moment—the sound of a summer shower raining down on the tree canopy; the soft indent of wet sand beneath her feet; and right now, most of all, the shine of Audrey's pale-blonde hair, curled out at the ends like it was trying to grow toward a light source.

"Will it eat us?" Audrey asked. She was lingering within the shelter of a tree copse. The expanse before them was a wide, exposed beachfront. The place where earth met ocean and the sounds of water and sand's fornication soothed human visitors.

"It only eats once a year that we know."

"The maiden?"

Verna smiled at Audrey in a way she hoped was reassuring. She didn't know if Audrey was a virgin or not, and frankly, Verna had long surmised that it didn't matter. But most young women refugees to the island feared they'd be chosen at Maiden's Feast if they had been chaste and so many, unlike Verna, rushed to fuck the nearest man they could find. Of course, most men were already coupled and so men took to taking on more than one wife at a time. Even so-called Christian men, practitioners of the old way from the mainland, "found it in their hearts" to sacrifice their bed to more than one woman if need be. It had been argued by a newcomer once that perhaps the sacrifice should be randomly selected, and not a maiden at all, but when the island Council suggested the dissenter be sent to Elogona, he suddenly decided a maiden was better after all for the sleepy water god.

Everyone and everything wanted to feast on women. Verna only wanted to love one.

"Who's to say if Elogona wants a maiden?" Verna asked.

"Well, the Council says she doesn't bother the fishermen if she takes a maiden once a year."

"The Council says lots of things. Did anyone ask Elogona what she wants? Does anyone know? Come."

Verna took Audrey's hand and led her onto the beach. She paused to take off her sandals, and gestured for Audrey to do the same. Audrey took off her shoes, exposing bright red painted toenails. It made Verna momentarily self-conscious—she'd never been good about keeping up with polishes and fashion. It was fortunate the two became less commonplace during the postwar years. She'd always focused much more on discourse than on appearances.

"Do you like them?" Audrey asked. She'd caught Verna staring.

"They're cute." Verna cleared her throat. "You know, if you're into that sort of thing." She could feel her face get hot at the lie—fact was, Audrey was downright gorgeous—but Verna also was consumed with the fear of scaring her away. Not many women spoke to Verna on the island because they either considered her a sinner who'd brought this hell upon them, or they worried she'd make a move on them. To have company like Audrey, who was letting her hair down with Verna, and who wanted to hear what she had to say, was rare. So rare that it filled Verna with a paralyzing fear of loss and ruin. If she let on that she thought Audrey was beautiful, would this be goodbye?

The wet sand gave way under their feet and they headed closer to the tide, which would be coming in soon. The low, deep thrum came up from the ocean. Many found it baleful, but Verna thought it was a lament. She related to Elogona; they were both lonely.

"My father says the beast is from Hell," Audrey said and she looked out at the ocean with a mixture of anger and fear. Her arms unconsciously rose up to hold herself. Verna thought about reaching out and cradling Audrey into her own embrace. She could protect her from Elogona; however, she could not protect her from men.

"They'll want to couple you soon," Verna warned.

"I don't want that." Verna thought she noticed Audrey hug herself tighter.

A breeze swept in the smell of salt, but also a tinge of decay and specks of ash—detritus in the air from the mainland. There would be more ships; there would be more refugees. Something the Council often discussed was when they should draw the line in the sand and accept no more. Land was getting crowded in the island's habitable parts.

"You're pretty though," Verna choked out the words. They burned like acid in her mouth—a vocal admission that she'd been looking. And she had. Audrey's face and physique were artfully formed, as if every feature were carved with vision and aesthetic sensibility. Her cheekbones were prominent, her nose symmetrical, her lips a mild pout in their natural state, so slyly downturned that they made her smile all the more radiant when it appeared. And her clavicle—the way it gracefully presented as a gateway to lower geography...She was a World unto her own.

"What's that got to do with anything?"

"If you're pretty, they'll want to couple you. They try to sacrifice the ugly maidens first if they can. Or, the noncompliant."

"And why aren't you coupled?"

Was Audrey asking because she was interested in Verna, or was she asking because she wanted to understand a survival strategy—a way out of having to spread her legs for some man?

"They tried. I resisted."

The tide came in, as if on cue, and laps of ocean water pooled around their feet. Audrey stepped back onto the sand as if stung and Verna let out a peal of laughter. She reached for Audrey's hand. "It's fine. You can come in the water."

Audrey shook her head. She was terrified.

"Well, I'm getting in," Verna declared. She threw off her blouse—a light, breezy blue tunic that hung off her shoulder, and waded into the ocean in denim shorts and a bleach-stained camisole she'd been wearing for far too long. The ocean was cool, and its constant undulations tickled her legs. Verna heard the sorrowful thrum of Elogona, even though she couldn't see the creature.

"Come back!"

Verna turned around and saw Audrey dancing in the ankle-high tide drift, lifting her feet up and down like the sand was on fire. It was an amusing sight.

Verna beckoned to Audrey to come in further and at first, she thought she'd convinced her. Audrey took a few more steps, letting the water lap up to her calves before she stopped. Verna could see her scouring the ocean, peering at it with suspicion.

It would be good to go back and comfort her. It was also good to show her that Verna did not fear the water. Verna did not fear the water because the men feared the water, and anything that the men feared could be a friend to women, or so Verna surmised.

Audrey trembled when Verna emerged from the ocean unscathed.

"You shouldn't do that. You shouldn't go so far out."

Verna grabbed Audrey's hand and led her back from the rising tide to a patch of sand under the shade of the palm copse. Verna laid back on her elbows and let Audrey look.

Elogona's music grew louder and carried over the waves.

"It sounds like an elegy, the kind they used to play at church."

Verna stared out at the boundless waters.

"When the war first broke, we thought we were safe for a time," Verna explained. "And then the refugees started coming from the mainland. We could see them by day—their little boats just dots on the water in the distance. But in the morning, limbs and carnage washed ashore."

"Elogona."

Verna nodded.

"I miss home," Audrey said. She ran the bottom curl of her hair through her two fingers as if she were straightening it.

Verna asked Audrey what home was like for her, and how it differed from here. Audrey told her about her mother, Isabelle, and how she was an elementary school teacher. How Isabelle would stay up late into the early morning hours arranging craft activities and packing snack bags for the kids who didn't have enough to eat in their lunch boxes. Audrey also told Verna how Isabelle burned alive when a missile hit the elementary school.

Tears cascaded, and Verna could see that there was a separate ocean within Audrey, as mystical and deep as the one surrounding the island.

"I'm sorry. I thought I was done crying about it." She wiped the rivulets from her cheeks and breathed in heavily—sucking in air like it would harden her against grief. There was no cure for human loss. Though she knew many men and women who found a salve in God, or as many on the island called it, Elogona.

Verna didn't believe in an afterlife. Maybe it existed. Maybe it didn't. But to believe in it wholeheartedly felt out of place. She believed in what she could hold in her hands, and see with her eyes. At that moment, she believed in worshiping at the altar of Audrey, sacrificing what she could in hopes a smile would return to her beautiful companion's face.

"I'm scared of the coupling," Audrey admitted.

"Have you ever had sex?"

Audrey blushed. She stretched out her legs and started kicking at sand with her feet, letting it fall between her toes. An anxious gesture.

"You shouldn't ask me that."

But Verna didn't care. She'd already won, because Audrey was smiling. A small smile, but it was a smile, nonetheless.

Audrey reached out and touched Verna's hand. Verna's heartbeat accelerated at the touch, but she willed herself to make eye contact.

"One day, I want to be brave like you."

Their first kiss was tender and quick. Verna feared she had to steal it quickly or else risk the chance of forever foregoing it.

The second kiss was longer and wet. Audrey didn't know what she was doing, but she held Verna's head to hers with earnest passion and curiosity.

It was okay. First and second kisses were never masterworks. They were messy, impromptu poetry.

When their heads parted and Verna ran a finger down the delicate slope of Audrey's pale shoulder, she saw him watching from behind a tree.

Councilman Hillard.

Hillard, realizing that he was caught, walked out from the trees with unmatched arrogance.

"Don't spoil yourself," the Councilman said and he

bent down to breathe in Audrey's face. Cupping her cheek in his unkempt hands, he forcibly turned her head toward the ocean. "Spoiled women don't couple, and if you don't couple, to the monster you go."

Elogona thrummed and the Councilman started humming his own sordid tune, a mockery of the organ-like music coming from the ocean.

"Leave her alone." Verna wished she'd said it with more confidence, but she knew well the immense and unbreakable power that Councilman Hillard held over his followers. He was, after all, the founder of Maiden's Feast. He figured out how to get Elogona to stop feeding constantly. His followers credited him with bringing back the fishing supply.

Fill a hungry man's belly, and he'll be loyal for a time. Fill the bellies of a hungry man's children and he'll kill for you. Councilman Hillard had many men on the island who would kill for him.

Verna grabbed Audrey's hand and pulled her away from Hillard. He sat down on the same plot of sand where the two women had been kissing moments ago, and it filled Verna with rage. Hillard was a predator who viewed women like fresh territory—something to be conquered, not loved. "Audrey has to get home for dinner," Verna said. She had to use most of her strength to hold up Audrey, who was overcome with anxiety and trembling.

When Verna dropped off Audrey at her parents' house—a small refuge made of wood and scrap, Audrey stopped her at the door. "I think it's best if you go home now," Audrey said. She couldn't meet Verna's eyes when the words left her mouth.

Verna ran a hand through her shaggy brown hair, speckled with sand and surf. She was too used to not wanting to be seen to be offended. "See you tomorrow then?"

Audrey looked around her and, seeing no one was watching, quickly landed a peck on Verna's cheek before running up to a hanging curtain that served as the door to her home.

The place where Audrey's lips had been on Verna's cheek felt electrified. She didn't want to touch the spot or else she might numb the sensation. Verna smiled the entire way home.

Verna's family lived on the main part of the island with the others, but three years ago, Verna's parents had tearfully asked her if she might consider living elsewhere, apart from people. Her mother had explained that the neighbors felt Verna brought a curse upon them and didn't want to be sharing the street with her.

The shack Verna called home really wasn't that different from the other refugee settlements on the mainland. It was made of mud, wood, and whatever scrap she could find that washed ashore. She liked being closer to the water and away from everyone, but it could also be lonely out on her own, and frightening. There were times in the night, where young men from the settlements would come and taunt her. Verna feared them, but she always pretended to not be afraid. She meditated on Elogona's distant song and envisioned herself as a stone upon still water. And Verna had a secret plan that she told no one—if it became too miserable here, if the men ever came for her—she would run into the ocean and give herself to Elogona. She would rather feed her body to a lonely ocean God than to a craven human man.

Hope kept her alive. It kept Verna going, as she curled up on her threadbare mat on the floor of her shack. Elogona was particularly mournful tonight and the elegiac tunes came in with the salt breeze. Verna remembered the time before the war—the time of libraries, cafes, aspirations, and schools. And as sleep approached even closer, she tried her best to recall the feel of Audrey's mouth on her skin, of Audrey's hair in her fingers.

WHEN AUDREY TOLD her brother Danny about Hillard appearing on the beach, he tensed up with anger.

"I have a bad feeling about this place," Danny said. Their father had left to see if there was anything of use from a recent scrap haul.

"Hillard gives me the creeps, Danny."

The two siblings were shucking corn. It was different from the corn they remembered from before the war. The ears had mottled husks, and their kernels were a sickly yellow that reminded Audrey of hospitals.

"Save the husks," Danny said. Audrey's brother was always devising ways to make use of scraps and refuse. It was an endearing trait before the war but now it was an essential skill, and she was grateful.

"You like her, don't you?" Danny prodded in the midst of their work. Audrey couldn't help but smile, despite efforts not to. Even though she and Danny shared almost everything with each other after Mom died, it was still hard to talk about personal crushes.

"I think she's kinda pretty," Audrey admitted without looking Danny in the eye.

Her brother nudged her playfully in the ribs, "Oh *kinda* pretty, huh? All it takes is *kinda* pretty for you to go off googly-eyed spending whole afternoons on the beach together?"

Audrey laughed, shoving his playful nudging away. "Okay," she confessed, "Verna is *really* pretty." Then, more seriously, "I can't stop thinking about her."

Danny pulled Audrey into a side hug. "It's nice to see you happy. After everything, even in this shit heap, it's nice to see a little happiness."

Audrey was scared of happiness. It was easier for Danny to be happy for her. He didn't realize the feeling inside of Audrey was fragile and blooming—on the verge of collapse, and out of her control. Audrey knew she had no way to stop the people here from shattering the joy she felt growing inside of her, and she felt terrified of it. There was a somber consideration deep inside to never see Verna again because Audrey was horrified by the thought of losing what was growing between them.

As if Danny could read her worries without her

having to voice them, he reassured her, "It's going to be okay. Nothing bad is going to happen."

They continued shucking the pitiful ears of island corn until they had a pile of discolored husks and a stack of ears ready for boiling. Even though it was a fairly tall stack, it wouldn't amount to much. And meat was hard to come by unless the Council provided it. Hillard and his cronies controlled the supply of fish. When the boats came in, it was the Council who got the first pick. There was always enough to feed the Council, their wives, their children, and their more ardent supporters. The newest refugees tended to get the last pick of the pile. For now, Audrey's family had to rely mostly on vegetables, roots, and the odd fruit. Meat was a luxury.

Voices filtered in through the shabby makeshift fabric door. One voice was their father's, but she could hear other voices mixing with his. Low, male tones cutting each other off until each voice was raised louder and louder in anger.

Audrey peeked through the curtain and saw Councilman Hillard standing opposite her father. Hillard had two other Council members and his first wife, Lisbeth, standing close by. He looked smug as ever, in contrast to her father, who had a pained, defeated expression on his face. She saw defeat in her father all too often after their mother died. Seeing what losing love had done to him—it made Audrey scared to embrace the feelings she had for Verna.

Audrey didn't have to wonder very hard what the men were fighting over. She knew it had to do with her.

She had seen the way Hillard had looked at her when she was sitting on the beach with Verna. She knew what he wanted, and it sent her stomach lurching. Hillard was much older, and he had a repulsive quality about him—whenever he was near, it was like he'd left a trail of ooze behind. An invisible slime, which seemed to coat over all he touched. She didn't want to be covered in that feeling. No, Audrey was resolved to stay as far away from Hillard for as long as possible.

Peeking from behind the curtain door, she strained to hear what they were saying. It wasn't lost on her how they were discussing her future, and how she wasn't at all involved in the discussion.

Danny stepped close behind her and also peeked around the curtain's edge. She worried about Danny even more than she worried for her father. Her brother was young and less controlled. He felt he could fight all of them off if he must. His desire to protect felt like both a gift and burden to Audrey. It made her feel responsible for his well-being.

"Fine," Hillard said, and Audrey glimpsed a sleazy look in his eyes. "If you don't want me to marry your daughter, then we'll have to put her to another use."

"What's that supposed to mean?"

"There's a beast that needs feeding, Mister Callum."

Even though Audrey knew Hillard was referring to the Elogona, she also couldn't help but think of Hillard as a monster, too. He had his own appetites, and his own way of quenching them.

Danny brushed past her through the curtain and

stepped out onto the dirt where Hillard and their father were squaring off. Audrey's heart beat fast in her chest.

"Is there a problem here, Hillard?" Danny refused to call him by his honorific, which Audrey could tell grated on the Councilman.

"There's always a problem nowadays," Hillard said cryptically. "It turns out, I'm in the business of solving problems."

"Only problem I see here is you," Danny spat.

"How dare you!" Lisbeth shrieked at Danny. Hillard's first wife was a ghoul who fervently clung to her feeble status.

"Well we never sacrificed a male virgin, but I'm willing to try it," Hillard quipped. His cronies laughed.

Danny grew red in the face and lurched at Hillard, only to be held back by their father.

"Forgive my son," their Dad said, with a vacant, sad stare.

Hillard stood back, his arms crossed, and an easy satisfaction on his face. Hillard had not been challenged in a long time; he was very comfortable in his power.

"You can have Audrey," their Dad said. "Forgive Danny, and you can have Audrey. If it means saving her life, you can have her."

"Dad, no!" Audrey's brother screamed.

Audrey could not believe her ears.

"You should be ashamed of yourself," Lisbeth scolded, "Marrying a Councilman is a high honor for your sister. More than she deserves. And forgiveness is more than you deserve."

Hillard held out a hand as a signal to his ghoulish first wife to say no more. "This isn't the place for you, Lisbeth."

Lisbeth sulked back behind Hillard, her dour face in its natural downturned expression, as if pulled by the depths of Hell into gloomy repose.

When Hillard had stalked off, with his cronies in tow, Audrey backed away from the fabric serving as a door. It took a lot of willpower for her to meet her father's gaze when he came inside.

Their father, who once seemed invincible, who was her hero when she was little—now was a shell of a man— a man hanging on by a thin, flimsy thread.

He didn't look at Audrey or Danny. He scrubbed at the dirt on the soles of his feet with a rag, and said, "It's all about survival now, kids. There's no want or wish. It's just about how to keep breathing."

VERNA WISHED she had a friend on the island. Someone to share her feelings with. She was brimming with emotion and excitement over the kiss she had shared with Audrey earlier on the beach, but there was no way to let any of it out. There only was the sound of Elogona, bleating its usual mournful song through blowholes. Elogona was so constant sometimes that the song faded into the background, as normal and expected as the wind blowing.

Verna laid down inside her shack and listened to the island's symphony. There was the sound of the sea beast, and the sound of the wind. A light rain hammered at her poorly thatched roof. Water leaked onto her body in rhythmic drops. It wasn't like the prewar rain—it was sour-smelling and if there was a bad drift from the mainland, it could burn. Verna crawled to a corner of her hut and covered her legs with mud to provide protection. It wasn't ideal, but it made do in a pinch.

And then, she thought of Audrey and Audrey's family. Verna remembered the day they had come in, and how Audrey had looked scared, how Audrey had clung to her brother's arm as they both ran from their boat onto the beach, covered in soot and sunburn. It would have been a traumatic scene if Verna hadn't seen it so many times before.

At least the Council hadn't killed them on sight, Verna thought. They did that sometimes when boats arrived with only men—a practice rarely discussed—but it was Audrey's beauty, shining through the long travel weariness—through the grime and ash—that had saved the Callums. Hillard had wanted Audrey from the moment he saw her.

At last, a merciful sleep came. When she awoke, Verna sat up with an ache in her stomach. The island was now one day closer to Maiden's Feast.

At least there were twenty-nine more days. Twenty-nine more days she could hopefully spend with Audrey on the beach, alone. Verna wanted to know everything about her. She wanted to know what her favorite foods were, and her favorite color, what her favorite book had been during the time when books were available, what her dreams were...

Verna decided to get up early and go shell hunting on the beach. Maybe she could find enough pretty little ones to string a bracelet together for Audrey. This fanciful thinking was cut abruptly short by a roar of mens' voices, and a screeching woman's howl. The howling—it was Verna's mother.

"Stop it! Wait!" Verna heard her mother scream. Verna opened the door. Members of the Council, led by Councilman Hillard, stood before her with makeshift batons in their hands. Behind them, trembling and crying, was her mother. Verna had never seen her mother look so terrified.

It was Hillard who spoke first.

"Girl, you know what you brought upon this place?"

Verna didn't say a word.

Councilman Tompkins held up a clear plastic bag. Verna felt sick upon seeing the contents—it was a mangled chunk of a leg, probably a woman's. Strips of flesh bobbed in the pooled blood at the bottom of the bag. The sight of it—the exposed bone and torn arteries—made Verna nauseous.

Hillard continued, "That's Jude Boykin's wife. What's left of her. She went out with Jude for a night fish last night and Jude claims the Elogona took her. That's what we have left."

"That has nothing to do with her!" Verna's mom screamed. Verna started to cry and hated herself for it, but her tears weren't coming from her own fear. They were coming from the sadness she felt at seeing her mother distraught.

Hillard smiled; he was pleased by the demonstration. "Oh but it does. I was elected to oversee this island and I've been keeping an eye on your daughter." Hillard spat in Verna's direction, but Verna didn't flinch.

"And I saw her last afternoon with that poor naive refugee, Audrey Callum. They were sinning. And even —" Councilman Hillard held up his finger for emphasis. "—and even if you don't think they were sinning, this abomination right here—" he pointed at Verna, "is preventing poor Audrey from saving herself. Who on earth is going to want to couple with Audrey after she's been with *that*?"

The other Councilmen murmured in agreement.

"But, I am charitable. And I talked to Audrey Callum's father. He begged me. Oh he *begged* me, to find a way to spare his daughter, to find a way to couple her. And even though I have seven wives, I decided to take an eighth." At this, Hillard stepped closer to Verna and looked deep into her eyes. Verna knew he wanted to feed off her pain. She tried to harden herself even though it felt like her heart had been cut open and was bleeding sorrow throughout her body.

Councilman Tompkins spoke again, "That's all well and good, Hillard, but somebody's got to pay for Boykin's wife."

The other men harrumphed and agreed.

Verna's mother flung herself between Verna and Hillard.

"I will pay," she said.

"The Elogona doesn't want some used up wife!" Tompkins shouted and the rest of the men laughed—all except for Hillard, whose slimy smile remained.

Verna grabbed her mother by the shoulders, her mom trembling as she pulled her into an embrace. The situation was dire, but Verna knew she had to be strong. Jean and Verna's relationship hadn't always been easy; there were times when Verna had thought she hated her mother for exiling her. But now, Verna only felt immense sorrow and regret.

Hillard spoke first, "The Elogona demands a maiden."

"How would you know! Can you understand its wailing?" Verna shouted.

"It spits back the pieces of women who aren't maidens. Chews them up and spits them out. Look at what remains of Boykin's wife."

Verna glanced again at what remained of Jude Boykin's wife. It was an awful sight. She didn't remember the woman well, but had seen her around the island.

"The Elogona wants a maiden and seeing as you're the only maiden around these parts that doesn't want to couple, then we've decided it should be you. Get you and your curse off our island once and for all."

Verna's mother broke out into a sob.

"This is a chance for you to do some good," Hillard said.

"This isn't fair," Jean cried out. Verna pulled her mother closer to her. She hadn't held her mother in so long, she didn't remember how small she was. Verna was the physically stronger of the two; living on her own had developed her muscles. Verna had learned to not rely on anyone for anything.

"It's okay, Mom," Verna said in a hushed whisper straight into her mother's ear. She stroked Jean's hair soothingly. Maybe it would be best if she went to Elogona, Verna thought sadly. In the belly of a water God, she could do no more harm. It would be safe there—restful. Verna would finally be able to be at peace.

But then the memory of Audrey's blonde hair sparkling in the sun came back to Verna.

No. She would find a way to survive. Verna always found a way to survive.

"Is there anything I can do to—to change your mind?" Verna choked out.

Hillard took a glance back at his old cronies, and they all shared glances and nods as if they'd had a previous discussion addressing Verna's question.

"You can couple with a man and leave behind your sinning ways. But you'd have to find a man willing to do it, and it would have to be done before Maiden's Feast."

"I won't do that," Verna said. Tears of rage spilled from her eyes, and an incandescent anger surged through her. She longed to tear out Hillard's tongue for all the poison it spoke across the island.

"It's your choice. You should thank your stars that we even give you a choice."

The men finally walked away, taking their time as they faded into the distance along the beachfront.

Only Jean and Verna remained.

"Verna, honey, sweetheart—" Jean began, but her voice cut off as she broke out into another sob.

"It's okay, mom. It's really okay. I know you tried."

Verna pulled her mom into a seated position on the sand, and they sat without speaking for a little while until Jean's sobs ran out and she was finally able to articulate a complete thought without choking up.

"I know you're scared of being with a man, but it won't be so bad. It'll mean keeping your life. Please. Will you do it for me?"

Verna's anger ballooned inside of her and threatened to burst. Even though it was against her natural inclinations, she wanted to hurt someone. She wanted to make everyone on the island feel her pain.

"*Scared* of being with a man? Is that what you think?"

"Honey, you have to give up this charade of kissing best friends and grow up. You're too old for this anymore! It's time to give it up and settle down."

"I'm never being with a man, except by force. And if by force, I'll slit that man's fucking throat."

"Verna!"

"I love women, Mom. And if it means they throw me to Elogona because of it, so be it. At least I'll die knowing who I am."

It was easy to say, but it was harder for Verna to

believe. Death scared her like it scared anyone else. She wanted to live. She wanted to build a house with Audrey and grow old on the beach together, but a different beach. Somewhere far away from here—a place without hurt and hatred. Did such a place exist? Was it possible?

"I'm scared for you, Verna. I'm so scared."

Verna wrapped an arm around her mother and wiped the tears from her eyes.

"Tell me a story of when I was a baby," she said.

Jean couldn't help but smile through her tears. "You haven't asked me to do that in a long time."

"Well, you don't come around here much."

Verna immediately regretted the barb. She knew her mom would visit more if she felt it were safe to do so, but it still hurt.

"When you were a baby, before the war, one of the first words you learned was 'happy'. And it's funny, your father and I spent so much time wondering *how did Verna learn that word* because we were busy teaching you 'mama' and 'dada'. But no, you learned 'happy'. And when I would lean close to you so you could see me, you'd reach out and touch my mouth and say *hap-py*. Your father and I just thought it was the best word in the whole wide world. We couldn't hear you say it enough."

Verna usually loved to hear about when she was a baby, but this time, it filled her with immeasurable sadness.

"Come on, Mom," Verna said as she got to her feet. She held a hand down for Jean and pulled her up. "I'll walk you home."

The walk back to her parents' house felt long. All Verna could think about was Audrey. She wondered if Audrey knew about Hillard's claim to her. The thought of Hillard's poisonous hands on Audrey's beautiful skin made Verna nauseous and enraged.

After dropping her mom off, Verna headed straight for the Callums' shack. She regretted not having anything to give Audrey when she arrived. There was something about Audrey Callum that made Verna want to do things for her. She briefly thought about the necklace she was going to make Audrey from beach shells, and decided it was just another reason to be angry at the stupid Council for interrupting her.

She stopped along the way and picked up some wildflowers, assembling them into a haphazard bouquet. As she walked, the people of the island turned their heads from her. Verna assumed word was getting around about what happened. Soon everyone would know Verna was going to be sacrificed at Maiden's Feast.

If Verna only had a couple of weeks left to be alive, then she knew for certain that she wanted to spend every one of them with Audrey by her side.

Danny, Audrey's lanky, good-natured brother, was outside of the Callums' ramshackle house when Verna arrived. He was trying to fix the siding and struggling with makeshift tools.

"Do you need help with that?" Verna asked, and she jogged up to lend a hand to the panel he was trying to hold in place.

"Hey, thanks," the young man said, and he flashed a shy smile at Verna.

"Is Audrey home?"

"She is... but..."

Before he could finish his sentence, Audrey ran out through the front curtain. All of Verna's worries paradoxically both faded and became more acute at the sight of Audrey. She was wearing a floral halter bathing suit top—the old kind from the prewar years, and some ripped shorts. Her blonde hair danced around her bare shoulders. Audrey kept running her fingers through it and the sight made Verna want to do the same.

"Danny, I'm going to go to the beach a little. Get some fresh air."

"You're not supposed to leave the house. Dad said."

"You know, Danny, those aren't the right kind of nails for a job like this," Verna winked at the kid and he blushed.

The remark made Audrey giggle, and for a moment it felt like they were somewhere else, sometime long ago.

"Alright, you two get out of here, but don't stay out too long, Audrey!"

Audrey and Verna ran off as quickly as they could. Verna didn't think she breathed during the whole run to the beach, she was so scared someone would interrupt them and take Audrey away.

"So, are those for me?" Audrey asked. She pointed at the droopy wildflower bouquet in Verna's hand.

Verna stretched her arm out with a smile. "Yeah. They're not the best, but here—" she grabbed an orange blossom from the mix and stuck the stem above Audrey's ear so that the flower decorated her blonde hair. "—that one suits you. It's beautiful."

"You look like you've been crying," Audrey said. She touched her slender finger to Verna's cheek. Verna rolled her shoulders and smirked. "Me, crying? Not a chance."

Audrey giggled. "Oh come on, like you don't cry ever?"

"Only when no one's around."

"Well, I brought something for you, too."

Verna's stomach flipped with anticipation. She hadn't received a gift from anyone in years.

Audrey pulled out a gold herringbone chain. "It was my mom's. I think it would look great on you."

Cupping her hand over the chain in Audrey's palm, Verna leaned down and looked into Audrey's eyes. "I can't accept this. It was your mom's."

"I can see it every time I'm around you."

"Audrey. Didn't you hear?"

Audrey waved her hand in the air as if she were shooing away a bad thought. "That's not going to happen. I'm not going to *let* it happen. Now take it."

Audrey showed surprising tenacity. There was a fierce spirit inside of her delicate, beautiful form, something Verna hadn't seen at first.

She took the sparkling golden chain from Audrey.

"Here, let me put it on for you."

Verna turned around and crouched down so that Audrey could see better; she was at least five inches taller than Audrey. Once the chain was clasped, Verna put her hand to it and touched the scaly-feeling herringbone.

"I don't think we should go to my place. I know somewhere quiet—somewhere no one will come looking for us."

Verna led Audrey by the hand as they walked along the coast to the northern side of the island. The northern side was flanked by steep, inhospitable cliffs—a harsh contrast to the sandy beaches on the southern coast. Nothing grew out by the cliffs and so it was unpopulated and quiet. The Council had deemed it uninhabitable. There was a treacherous path leading down the northern rock face to a small plot of beach that got flooded during high tide. It was there where Verna had found the cave a year ago during her solo explorations. It was risky to bring Audrey there—the path was not safe—and high tide sometimes came at unpredictable times, but it was the only place Verna was certain no one on the island would find them.

"I haven't been here before," Audrey said. It was colder on the northern side, and the salt-soaked wind whipped Audrey's blonde hair back from her shoulders.

"You don't have to come if you don't want to. I won't lie—this path is not the safest."

"You won't let me fall."

Their hands interlocked and Verna took the lead so she could support Audrey as they descended. It was fortunate the cliffs were dry, but the fierce wind threatened to knock them off balance.

Verna loved it out here. The ocean was wilder on the

northern side of the island, like the waves were dancing while no one was looking. The sea froth gathered and receded at the beach plot below and by the time Verna's toes touched the sand again, she felt a satisfying victory. They'd made it.

"Are we going in there?"

The cave presented a jagged reverse-U-shaped entrance into the cliffside, a dark interior completely obscured.

"It's a little dark but we'll stay near enough to the entrance that our eyes will adjust."

Audrey didn't want to go into the cave. It was hard to be convinced to leave behind the bright, sunny beaches and to go into the dark depths of a cavern. The human mind could conjure up all sorts of horrors when it stared into a dark opening.

Audrey came from bright city lights and bustling streets—until the war hit, at least. But even the mainland after the war was different from the island. In the midst of the mainland's devastation, there was still the echoing memory of civilization. That echo spread the hope that it could return.

Here, the island was like a castaway, a last bastion. It reminded all who lived here that all was lost, and that the settlement was all that remained. A floating piece of earth circled by an ancient beast.

There was danger in being on the northern shore. The tides were unpredictable in the postwar years. Whereas science used to hold them down to a particular minute of the day, now the tides could change patterns suddenly even after weeks of holding the same schedule. If the high tide came in, it could cover the cave entrance without warning and drown them both. Verna hadn't told Audrey that prior to hiking here, but somehow she saw in Audrey's eyes that Audrey knew anyway. It was now common knowledge between the women that their very act of being together was a possible death sentence. Verna reflected how it was strange to want to be near someone so much that you were willing to risk your own life—that you were willing to risk not ever being able to touch *anyone* ever again.

Verna couldn't explain why she felt the way she did about Audrey. There was wonder in the timing of their relationship, in that Audrey arrived on the island when Verna was at her lowest. There were many lonely nights that Verna spent in exile—nights spent counting the few stars that appeared in the polluted sky.

If Verna were being honest, she had more than one reason to bring Audrey to the cave. Sure, she wanted to be close to her and run her fingers through Audrey's pale blonde hair. But more than that, she wanted to see if the rumors were true.

There were rumors on the island—hushed rumors— that an old witch lived in the cave. When Verna heard the rumor, she dismissed it, but the more the rumors spread, the more the Council tried to silence them. The Council's efforts to suppress the knowledge led Verna to take much more stock in the tale than she would have otherwise.

"I'll go first," Verna said, "And you hold onto the back of my shirt."

"This reminds me of when I was a kid and my friends and I went to a haunted house. I pulled on my friend's shirt so hard, I almost choked her."

Verna laughed. "Now the whole world feels haunted, doesn't it?"

"What if something's in there?"

"Like what?"

"I don't know. Just... something? Like a spider?"

"Audrey. There are spiders all over this damn place."

"Yeah but what if there's a big one."

Verna made a crawling motion with her fingers across Audrey's bare shoulder, and it sent Audrey into a fit of giggles. She squirmed and shuddered. Verna had long dispensed with any fear of bugs. Living in the postwar years on the island meant learning to share space with hundreds of insect varieties. They were more resilient than humans, and Verna was sure that it would be a fly or a cockroach that outlived the last human soul on earth.

Verna took a step into the dark recess and had a moment of hesitation. She hadn't told anyone where they were going—they'd only told Audrey's brother Danny that they'd be gone for a bit. But they hadn't taken the time to share where. If they had disclosed their destination, Verna was sure that Danny would've protested. Danny was a well-intentioned young man who wanted what was best for his sister. But there was also something about him that seemed kind. He had, after all, smiled as he saw Audrey walking off with Verna, and that merited some praise. It wasn't easy being a new refugee and it especially wasn't easy being connected to Verna. She was a pariah. And she was sure that when Councilman Hillard came to Mr. Callum's house to talk about marrying Audrey, that the Councilman presented in no uncertain terms what an abomination he found Verna to be.

But Verna knew a secret about Councilman Hillard. She remembered when he had come on to her, and shuddered at the memory.

"Verna, can you see anything?"

Verna returned her attention to the cave. They were now a few steps beyond its ominous entrance. It took a moment for their eyes to adjust but eventually Verna was able to distinguish some rock formation outlines in the dark haze.

"See, it's not so bad. It's like being in bed with the lights off. Your eyes adjust."

"You have no idea how much I'd kill for a comfy bed."

"I'll make you a bed."

"What's the use if I'll have to share it with a man?"

"You won't."

Verna drew Audrey close to her and they fell to the rocky floor in an embrace. She didn't want their afternoon together to be soiled by the looming doom that hung over them. Verna wouldn't let Audrey marry Councilman Hillard, no matter what.

"What do you know about him?"

"He's a monster. I know that much."

"I mean, I gathered as much. But why does he have so much power here?"

"He was one of the Kensington Thirteen."

"The Kensington Thirteen?"

"Yeah. They were a group of preppers who had marked this island on a map as their bug-out location in case of worldwide calamity—war, plague, you name it. So, they were the first to arrive. They arrived here way before most of the mainland thought about trying to escape. And as you know, by the time most people started thinking about leaving the mainland, there weren't enough ways to get out, or many safe places to go."

"Who's the Kensington Thirteen? Councilman Hillard and who else?"

"Oh only four survive. Hillard. Tompkins. Martindale. Allen."

"What happened to the rest?"

"Did you really want to come all the way here with me just to talk about decrepit old men?"

Audrey's giggles echoed throughout the expansive space. It made Verna uneasy for a moment as she thought about the rumors of the witch. Was there something lurking in the darkness? Would Audrey's lovely giggles draw the monster out from the depths? Verna couldn't place why she thought it was worth verifying if the rumors were true. Maybe it was because Verna sympathized with a creature or human so lonely as to spend a lifetime stuck away in a dark cavern on the northernmost side of the island, where no one wanted to go because of how inhospitable it was.

"Elogona ate the rest. That was before the time of Maiden's Feast."

Audrey shuddered. Verna could tell that Elogona scared Audrey very much.

"I'd heard about the beast before my father took us here. I was terrified of crossing the ocean, and we didn't have a large boat. I had nightmares on the open sea that I'd wake up and be swallowed by the massive jaws of a beast from beneath. Even during the day, I thought at any moment that perhaps our small vessel would disappear and be swallowed up by the ancient vermin."

"I'm glad that didn't happen."

Verna pulled Audrey in closer and swept hair out from her face. Verna felt Audrey's breath on her neck. They kissed. Verna wished she could kiss Audrey for all eternity.

Something stirred in the darkness. Verna wondered if it were bats, perhaps, or cave crickets.

"Did you hear that?"

The sound of wings—or was it legs—rubbing together. Was it a bee? An insect? The sound became louder and louder. Audrey pressed herself hard against Verna, almost burrowing herself into Verna as if she thought she could hide inside her girlfriend.

A small globule of sharp green light bounced from a cave tunnel toward the antechamber, like a kid's rubber ball. It bounced on the stone floor, up and down, up and down, until finally landing in front of Verna and Audrey.

Slowly it illuminated the cave's interior until everything was visible, displayed in a vibrant emerald green shade.

"That's better," crooned a voice. The sound of legs rubbing against each other became clearer and closer.

Verna and Audrey both looked up at the same time and shrieked.

Hanging on the ceiling above them was a creature unlike any Verna had ever seen. It did not look how she imagined a witch would look at all, and in fact, she could not be sure if this was the rumored witch of the island. She was sure, however, that the creature was utterly terrifying. It had a head with six eyes, and a human-like mouth, but there was something uncanny about its lips. The uncanniness was elucidated as Verna and Audrey watched the creature's jaws unhinge—a sticky, white-dotted muscled tongue extending downward toward them until it rested its spiny tip on Verna's forehead before retracting sharply.

"Too sweet," the creature whined, and then extended its tongue again but this time toward Audrey. As the tongue came closer and closer, Verna moved to cover Audrey so that its spiny tip jabbed into Verna's back.

The tongue retracted again and the creature, temporarily thwarted, skittered down from the ceiling in a fluid flurry of legs that left Verna shaken.

"Get us out of here," Audrey whispered.

The weevil-like witch scurried toward the two women and took them in with its six eyes.

"You come to my cave and won't give me a taste?" Its hard carapace, shiny in the green light, fluttered a few of its scales. They opened and closed, making unsettling clinking sounds.

"You can't taste her," Verna said stoically.

"And why's that?"

"What are you?" Audrey asked the question with disgust and shock. The forcefulness of her voice surprised Verna, who thought Audrey might've been rendered mute by sheer terror.

The weevil witch tittered. Its uncanny lips spread into a perturbed smile. Verna hated looking at its mouth, illuminated in the ghastly green light, knowing the thick, knotty length of spike-tipped tongue that hid inside.

"I am the Mervosa, the witch that crawled from the sea. What are you? I hope you are far more savory in flavor than your friend."

"We are not food," Audrey insisted, "And you look like no witch I've ever seen."

The weevil witch's lips turned from smile to something strange—a disfigured angle like a quizzical scar.

"But you can't have seen any witches like me."

"I've seen them plenty in books," Audrey said, with such naivete that it made Verna's heart swell and fear all the more.

"Those aren't witches," the Mervosa cackled. "Those are figments of imagination, thought threads spun into paper trash. You can't have seen any witches like me, Tasty," the Mervosa said. It skittered closer, "Because I am the last one."

Its tongue lashed out from its mouth and this time managed to prick Audrey's bare shoulder with its spindly tip. The layered shells of its carapace fluttered open and closed in some kind of intoxicated jubilee.

Verna pulled Audrey back in horror, but as they retreated, the Mervosa's tongue extended even farther, to such a great length that Verna wondered if the entirety of its insides were composed of tongue tissue, coiled tightly like a spring and waiting to extend.

Audrey howled with disgust and beat the tongue with a balled-up fist.

The Mervosa retracted the tongue again, but skittered even closer, its six eyes lit up with delight in the green haze of its mysterious light globule, which continued bouncing and glittering in the background.

"Ah Tasty, you'd make a great chomp." Its many legs undulated like a wave, as if it were jolted and excited by the presence of Verna and Audrey. "I'd chomp your little limbs first, and suck the marrow out of those bones. How'd you like to spend some time with me alone? Get rid of that sickly sweet thing you travel with, so sugary she's like a disease."

"Keep away, witch," Verna warned.

Verna would do anything to keep Audrey safe.

"Yes, keep away," Audrey hissed, and Verna found herself impressed by the vehemence in Audrey's tone. "Keep away or we'll push you out to sea."

Audrey pointed to the water coming in—the tide was rising.

"I come from the sea, Tasty," the Mervosa said, almost purring.

"Yes, but there's a reason you left. You know what's out there. The—"

"Don't say that name," the Mervosa said, and Verna could tell that Audrey's words had gotten under its shell, and had nestled a little hole in its monstrous confidence.

"Why not? Elogona. Elogona, Elogona, Elogona!"

The Mervosa hissed and skittered backwards, its green globule of light bouncing with it until both were on the side of the cavern opposite Audrey and Verna. Ocean water began to pool around Verna and Audrey's ankles. The Mervosa, its insectile body parallel to the two lovers, swung up its head and stared at them with greenly illuminated eyes. "How dare you come here and mention that devil's name. The devil who killed the sea witches."

The beast stopped speaking as Elogona's mournful music floated over the rising ocean tide.

"What do you want?" hissed the sea witch. "Why are you here? Did it send you here, is that it? Did it send you here to take me?"

"Yes, it sent us here to take you to it. Everyone knows how much Elogona loves to eat sea witches. And if you take me or harm me—Verna—the one you call diseased, will run for the hills and she'll tell all the other people where you are. They'll come with their nets and spears, and they'll drag you out in a burning ship to perish on the open sea, unless Elogona opens its jaws for you first."

The ocean water was now up to Verna and Audrey's calves, and small minnows began to swim in with the tide. The Mervosa jutted its tongue out and lapped up a small fish from the ocean, swallowing it whole. The beast's deceptive mouth screwed itself back into a small purse before emitting an acidic, satisfied belch.

"Salty."

Verna suddenly had an idea. As much as she was shocked at how easily Audrey could lie and worm her way out of this predicament, and as guilty as she felt for leading poor Audrey into the Mervosa's lair, she also found an opportunity.

"What if we did you a favor, though."

"A favor?"

"Helped you," Verna offered.

The Mervosa laughed, its carapace shells opening and closing in delight. "How can a little wretch like you help me?"

"Easy. We'll tell Elogona that we couldn't find you. You see, it thinks you're hiding here but it can't get here itself, so it convinced us to come searching for you on its behalf. It said that if we could capture and feed you to it, that it would grant us safe passage over the ocean, and that we would be spared from the next Maiden's Feast."

The Mervosa seemed to consider the explanation.

"And what would you want from me? What would you want in return for telling it I'm not here?"

Verna looked at Audrey's beautiful face in the cave's green light.

"There's a man who wants to marry Audrey and we can't have that. We need him gone. We need to get out of it somehow before Maiden's Feast happens. If we can get him here, to the cave, can you help us?"

"Well that depends," The Mervosa said.

They waited a moment to hear the creature's demands.

"Is he tasty?"

By the time they swam out of the cave, the ocean tide was up to their hips. Verna worried the current might take them away from the cliff path. It was much harder to get a foothold during high tide. Verna feared they would slip and fall into the ocean. If they wouldn't be eaten by Elogona, then surely they would drift back into the U-shaped cave entrance, right into the Mervosa's lair. Verna would be spared because she didn't taste to the witch's liking, but Audrey would be eaten in one swift swish of the thick, muscular tongue. The touch of the sea witch's spindly tongue on her forehead would haunt her dreams for some time.

Audrey looked worse for wear, like she'd run a long distance and hadn't eaten. This wasn't exactly the nice, romantic afternoon that Verna had planned for them in her head. The climb up the cliff was treacherous, made even more so by the ferocious lapping waves beneath. If Audrey's father knew where they were—if Councilman Hillard knew—Verna was sure they would throw her out to sea that very night. They wouldn't wait for the Maiden's Feast. They'd find another poor woman to sacrifice at that time, and swiftly kick Verna to the curb. Verna had caused enough problems, in their mind, and they didn't understand her. They didn't understand why she wasn't an Eloganite and wasn't a Christian, why she kept to herself, why she didn't want to couple. No one understood her but Audrey—sweet, intelligent Audrey, who cleverly lied to the Mervosa and saved both their hides from a chomp. The thought made Verna shudder.

So, the rumors were true, Verna thought as they finished the climb. She had to pause to wait for Audrey to catch up on many legs of the climb because Audrey was far less muscular than she was, and seemed to be crashing from a post adrenaline rush. Verna imagined that when Audrey was told she was going to be eaten by the sea witch, that her body was inundated with fight-or-flight hormones. Now that she was out of the cave, Audrey's body had plummeting energy levels, depleted from all the force it took her to outsmart the monster.

Verna was ashamed to think she had thought of a sea witch as something she had seen from storybooks long ago—perhaps a woman with a strange hat, and a pot with bones in it. Instead, it was a monstrous insect humanoid creature unlike anything Verna could have dreamt up even in her nightmares. She shuddered to imagine that she had been sharing the same island with that thing all this time, and didn't know it.

The Eloganites believed that the fall of man precipitated the rise of ancient hellish beasts, who came to take dominion over earth again. They were major and minor gods, as befitting their powers and positions, according to the cultists. The Christians, however, believed that most of the rumors of beasts and monsters were myths, with exception to Elogona, who was a creature of God, sent to be punitive for the sins of man. Both worshiped the beast in their own strange way, but Verna now felt more respect for the Eloganites, who seemed to have at least unlocked the knowledge that there were more beasts and creatures than just the sea monster.

Verna found herself wondering what else was out there, and if monsters were stalking the mainland as well. She asked Audrey as much when they finally reached the top of the cliffs. A cold rain poured on them as they walked south, the wind and rain turning their already ocean-soaked bodies frigid.

Seeing how cold Audrey was, and how she shivered, Verna decided to pull Audrey under the shelter of nearby palm trees. Verna pressed Audrey against the largest tree trunk, the expansive fronds providing the most cover, and proceeded to rub Audrey's sides vigorously, pressing against her to generate body warmth. The closeness was more intimate than sexual—a practical necessity in their strange circumstances—and as soon as the rain started to ease up, their grip on each other loosened. The sun peeked out from behind the storm clouds and Audrey smiled for the first time in hours.

"We met a sea witch, Verna. And she's going to save me from that awful man."

Verna shushed Audrey, and explained in a soft tone that now that they were getting closer to the south side settlements, they should watch what they say. Verna was often followed or stalked by The Council's cronies, and she didn't want anyone to hear about the Mervosa or their plan to bring Councilman Hillard to the witch. Verna, herself, still didn't fully understand how they were going to pull off the plan. All she knew was she had to find a way to get it done before Maiden's Feast, or else Councilman Hillard would try to take Audrey for his own. The thought of that old bastard's hands all over Audrey's delicate skin made Verna want to break something.

When they got close enough to the settlements, with lines of ramshackle houses in sight, Verna and Audrey decided to part ways. Fearful of watching eyes and who might report what to The Council, they decided to forego any goodbye embrace and instead locked eyes with each other for a long moment. Verna wished, in that moment of connected gaze, for a world where they could say goodbye as affectionately as they wanted, and without the judgment of others.

As Verna walked back to her exile, she reminisced over the feel of Audrey's body. The feel of Audrey's curves pressed against Verna's toned frame. How Audrey's softness felt so good against her taut muscles, and how she only wanted to lavish Audrey with affection and care. She daydreamed about the two of them back on the mainland before the war hit. In an apartment, fancy that. With their own bed, and a view. A city view, even. Far away from the ocean, and Elogona—and far away from the knowledge of the Mervosa, in a world where the only insects and skittering things were easily dealt with under the sole of a shoe. Verna would give anything to change the order of time and somehow be born earlier, meet Audrey earlier, in another world, where they could've loved each other in a way that wasn't stipulated by the minds of power-hungry men.

Of course, intruding on all her lovely wishes and daydreams about Audrey, was the horrific consideration that Councilman Hillard might set his hands on her at any moment. By the time Verna reached her home, she had a plan for how she could lure the Councilman away from the settlements to the sea witch's cave.

It would be dangerous, but it was her only chance.

II

When Audrey got back to her house, Danny was sitting on the stoop. She was awash with confusion and wonder. She wanted to go into her own room and relive what had happened that afternoon with Verna, but seeing Danny's warning expression, she knew something was up. And besides, she had no room of her own anymore. They'd left all that behind when they decided to come to this dreadful place. The only good thing about the island settlement was that she and Danny and Dad were still together—the way Mom would have hoped—and that she had met Verna. Verna was special. She made Audrey feel seen for the first time in a very long time.

Audrey's family was way more accepting of Audrey's sexuality than Verna's family was of hers, but they knew the culture of the island, and they knew what the world had become. They knew that if Audrey was at all open about how she felt, that she would be exiled like Verna, and poor Dad didn't want to see that happen to his only daughter.

"They're waiting inside," Danny said. He looked sad even as he said it, as if he regretted that it had to be so.

Audrey groaned and opened the door. Danny was right behind her, and he put a hand on her shoulder for support. Danny was good-natured like that. He always wanted to help.

Inside, Audrey saw Councilman Hillard and his first wife, Lisbeth Hillard, sitting on their only two chairs while poor Dad sat in a squat on the floor. He looked tired—and defeated.

Lisbeth tsked at the sight of Audrey, giving her a once-over from toe to sternum in a way that screamed disapproval. Councilman Hillard, on the other hand, drank Audrey in slowly and leeringly, in such a shameless way that everyone in the room noticed. Audrey blushed in embarrassment. She suddenly wished she had worn something more modest than a halter top, and she worried about her breasts showing through the wet fabric. She hated how the Councilman looked at her. Frankly, he scared her.

Male gaze had always felt like a residue she didn't deserve and couldn't wash off.

Lisbeth also scared Audrey. She was mean-faced and unpleasant. She looked sour and like she wanted to yank Audrey by the hair, if given the chance.

Danny wrapped an arm around Audrey and pulled her closer to him, a protective gesture. Dad offered a weak smile to them both. Audrey could see that he had been bulldozed by the Council, that he didn't want to give Audrey up, but also didn't know what else to do to preserve their family.

"Where have you been?" Councilman Hillard asked.

"I was just taking a walk. Searching for wild-flowers."

Lisbeth rolled her eyes. "Searching for wildflowers? That sounds like a waste of time when there's so much work to be done."

Hillard hushed his wife, and she looked even angrier for it.

"Who were you walking with?" Hillard asked. The question was so pointed and acidic that Audrey feared Verna was right and that The Council had been watching them, stalking their movements. Hopefully they hadn't seen them go into the Mervosa's cave. She wondered how long they had followed them, and if they had seen their kisses, their caresses. Audrey felt violated. Like there was nowhere to go where she could just be herself in peace.

So, she chose not to lie to the old man. She wasn't going to play his games if he already knew who she was with that day.

"Verna."

Lisbeth gasped, appalled. "And you want to marry this sinning whore?"

Danny thrust a finger at Lisbeth, "Don't you dare call my sister a whore!"

That caused Hillard to likewise thrust a hand toward Danny, "And don't *you* speak up to my wife!"

It was Dad who stood up, arms in the air, and urged the room to calm.

"I think we could all do without the anger," Dad said, and Audrey watched as the room simmered. Lisbeth oozed dissatisfaction, and Audrey knew that if everything in her and Verna's hands went sour, and Audrey had to marry Councilman Hillard, that Lisbeth would make Audrey's life a worse living hell than it already was.

"I see you like to play kissing games with girls. That would disturb most men, but I've been known to have a lenient hand. I have seven wives, and some of them play kissing games with each other. So long as I'm invited, I don't care." He let out a bellow of a laugh, his own sick humor that no one participated in. The room was quiet, uncomfortable. The tension was miserable, like a prison unfolding over Audrey—an inescapable fate. Maybe she should've just let herself be taken by the sea witch. The Mervosa's spiked tongue was better than the horror of Councilman Hillard's leathery hands, and his wife's scornful face.

She knew her father was pressed for options, but her rage still simmered at him for agreeing to this. Mom would never have agreed. Mom would've found a way out. Or maybe that was a child's thinking, Audrey sadly considered. She thought of the herringbone necklace she had given Verna, and how it sparkled against Verna's tanned chest. The flutter in her heart at the image contrasted with her sharp disgust of seeing Councilman Hillard.

"In any case, the Maiden's Feast draws near and if

you're to marry a member of the Council, you'll need an Inspection, hear?"

Danny bristled. He protectively wrapped an arm around Audrey. "What kind of inspection?"

"The Council Wives will have to verify that she's pure, of course."

Dad blanched, but whether in shame or emasculation, Audrey couldn't tell.

"They'll do no such thing," Audrey said firmly.

"You don't have a choice in the matter."

"You can't make me."

Verna didn't know what to do with herself as soon as she had formulated the plan to foil Hillard. It was like when she was a child and a holiday was approaching—there was an excitement of anticipation, but also a lingering background anxiety that somehow the day would never arrive.

The only way for her to stop thinking about the impending plans was to try to occupy herself and bide the time—a task made all the easier as soon as the boat appeared in the distance.

More refugees, Verna thought.

Unfortunately for the boat, the day brought turbulent weather. Weather changed rapidly on the island, something both religious factions attributed to their alleged piety when the weather was good, and to Verna's sins when the weather was bad. Today, it looked like Verna had sinned. She laughed bitterly as the wind twirled around her, warm and thick with moisture.

Debris on the beach floated up with the stormy drifts, and scuttled down the shoreline as the ocean began roiling, receding, and attacking the island in violent bursts. The sky turned the color of bruised flesh and opened itself to pour foul-smelling rain—some of it acidic—down on them all.

The poor boat struggled to stay afloat on uneven waves. The vessel—only a small smudge on the horizon—swayed back and forth, and Verna could imagine the fear of its passengers. They'd probably spent great care to build the vessel, or to find one, and had finally taken their trip across the ocean, knowing full well the beast that swam beneath.

Verna stood in the pouring rain as she watched the boat flail on the horizon line. She stood and watched until she heard the massive groan of organ pipes from beneath the sea. It was the Elogona. There would be no refugees arriving today.

The acidic rain stained Verna's tunic and caused the skin of her arms to break out into small red welts. She knew she should go back inside her hut, but she couldn't help but keep watching. She had to see it for herself.

Soon the ocean formed a blackened rift—foamy wave crests made steep walls on either side of a terrifyingly dark trench. It wasn't a trench, at all, but Elogona's jaws, so wide as to appear as another island itself when it touched the surface of the ocean. The smudge on the shoreline— that poor, pitiful remnant of humankind—wobbled back and forth along the ocean water, now somewhat more still within the sanctity of the beast's jaws, until Elogona snapped them shut and retreated back to the depths, one more boatful of refugees in its cavernous belly.

There was no music for a time, and Verna returned to a semi-sheltered position under the eaves of her shack. Her skin burned and the storm wind whipped her shaggy brown hair into a frenzy. She thought of Audrey, and daydreamed about them sailing out from this place together.

Closing her eyes, Verna could see Audrey's blonde locks in the bright sun, sparkling and reflecting light at all angles. The two of them on a raft, tunics overhead on makeshift poles to provide shade. Oh it was a silly dream, Verna knew, but she clung to it behind her eyelids. She clung to it until she heard Elogona's pipes blow once more.

There's no way they'd make it off this island alive. Not with that beast out there.

The excitement that Verna had felt only moments before the storm—the anticipation of trying her hand at thwarting Hillard—was now dampened and drowned out by rain, trash on the wind, and the sound of footsteps running closer.

She looked up and saw Danny—good ole' Danny— running toward her. The poor guy was soaked through to the bone, but he kept on running and even had a smile on his face.

"What are you doing out here?" She called to him.

"You know, I could say the same of you."

"Get inside," she said, pushing him into her hut where they were shielded from most of the rain, but not all. Danny's skin looked as bad as hers, and she felt guilty that he'd exposed himself to the acidic storm just to come see her.

"Is Audrey alright?"

"She's alright, but I don't know how much longer I can stand seeing her like this."

Verna knew what Danny meant. It was part of the reason Verna both longed to be around Audrey and also feared it right now. There was so much riding on Verna's ability to carry out her plan to get rid of Hillard. The stakes of Audrey's sanity were held in the grip of Verna's competence, and it was almost too much to bear.

"I worry this is my fault," Verna admitted. "He hates me. I sometimes worry that he saw I loved her, and he immediately wanted to take her just to get at me. To hurt me."

"This is not your fault. This is no one's fault but Hillard's and everyone else who lets him have this power."

"Why'd you come all the way out here, Danny?"

"I saw the storm and I wanted to make sure you were alright. You mean a lot to my sister, you know. I have to make sure you don't die out here."

The young man's self-confidence in his ability to

protect Verna made her smile. There was something still so innocent about Danny's belief that he could change the world. She had to admit, it was refreshing. It reminded her there was life and hope beyond the swirling ash and gloom.

"I'm okay. I've been out here on my own for a long time now. I know how to take care of myself."

"Then why were you standing out there under this awful rain? If I can even call it rain."

"It's rain. Acid rain, we call it. There's hope that one day the normal rain will fully return. It leaves a rash, but it's worse for children than it is for us adults. For us, the rash fades quickly enough. And besides, who wants to go the rest of their lives without feeling rain on your skin? Even if it does burn a little."

"I sometimes wonder if there's anything worth living for anymore, Verna, and then I see you and Audrey and I know there is. You know that?"

Verna smiled at Danny.

"Love is always worth living for."

"And dying for. That's what you want to say, isn't it?"

Danny looked hard at Verna. He then added, "I know you both have some kind of plan. I'm worried. I don't trust that man not to do something bad."

"Oh if there's something bad to be done, Hillard will do it." Verna laughed morbidly.

"I'm serious, Verna. I'm worried sick about you both. I can't lose my sister." Verna realized Danny was about to cry, and she reached out and pulled him close to her. They had grown closer than Verna could ever have imagined they would; Danny was like a brother to her, as well. She knew how important Audrey was to him, and this was a feeling they shared and bonded over.

"I'm not going to let anything bad happen to your sister. I promise."

"I'm not sure that's a promise you can keep."

A tear rolled down Verna's cheek. He was right.

Lightning cracked outside. Verna and Danny sat quietly embracing each other as the storm raged on, the sound of the ocean beating the island a strangely sympathetic parallel to their own weltering emotions.

They waited until the storm died down for Danny to leave. Verna told Danny to tell Audrey that she was thinking of her, and that this would be over soon. Danny said he would. When Danny was at the entrance to their hut, Verna called out to him, "Wait!"

She then took a paring knife and cut off a lock of her salt-stained brown hair. She took a piece of old fishing line and tied it together before giving it to Danny. "Will you give this to her?"

Danny said he would.

Verna was sad to see Danny go. She liked to spend time with him almost as much as she liked spending time with Audrey. She wished they could all be together, but she knew that the Council had such a close eye on Audrey, there was no chance of it.

Verna blew softly on her arm welts to soothe them. She stepped outside onto the beach and took in the sight of the ocean. There were no more boats on the horizon, and the swell of the waves had calmed considerably. That was like the weather—it was capricious. One minute, it would be quiet and sunny—deceptively calm. The next, it was a violent storm of rain, wind, and squalls. They had no weather forecast to guide them here. Everything was left up to fate, or chance, depending on what you believed.

Verna knew the stakes of what lay before her. The specter of death had hung over her head since she'd arrived, even back to the days of the Kensington Thirteen, when the island was scarcely populated and there was still a sense of hope. Of something 'better'. But now, the sense of impending doom was somehow more real. There was a heavy dread in her bones. She hadn't wanted to tell Danny. He was too bright-eyed, too hopeful. She worried he wouldn't be able to take what she sensed would befall them all.

It's just a silly feeling, she thought. There was something heavier to it, though, that settled inside of her, like dominos falling that could not be put back upright. Since she and Audrey had left the sea witch's cave, Verna wondered if perhaps the sea witch had planted that feeling of doom. After all, she did not know the creature's powers and did not trust the witch to reveal the extent of them.

The sense of foreboding was ever acute, and Verna decided it was high time to visit her parents in the settlement. In the best case, she would succeed against Hillard, but in the worst, she would be submitted to the same fate as the refugee boat only hours previous—to the unforgiving belly of Elogona.

Either way, it was time she said goodbye to her father and mother. She knew her mother loved her, but could not say the same about her father. He was a weathered, simple man, sometimes so straightforward and unemotional that Verna wondered how she could be made from him. She sensed that to her father's eyes, Verna was also a strange creature, something he couldn't—no, *wouldn't*—understand.

She made her way to the settlement, wet to the bone with clothes clinging to her body and bringing on a chill. It had been so long since she'd stopped by their house for a visit, and the last time she'd seen her mother was when her mother had urged her to couple with a man to avoid the Maiden's Feast.

At least her mother *cared* to urge her, she thought bitterly. Her father hadn't spoken to her in years—not since the exile.

It was tempting to stop at the Callums' shack along the way, but Verna resisted the temptation. She headed onward to her parents' house, with its precious metal siding—a luxury not given to newcomers. Her parents even had a functioning wooden door, which was usually reserved for houses containing the Council.

Verna rapped her knuckles on the door and waited. It was scary to be there after so long away—a realization that filled her with heavy sorrow. No one should feel this scared to go home, she thought.

Finally, her mother answered the door. It looked like Jean had been crying for a very long time, with streaks down her sand-caked face.

"Who is it?" Verna could hear her father yell out from inside.

"It's no one," Verna's mother said, and Verna watched as fresh streaks flowed down Jean's sand-coated cheeks. New tracks of sorrow and misery.

"Mom?" Verna mouthed quietly.

But Jean just shook her head and closed the door in Verna's face.

To her parents, Verna was already dead. A walking ghost they'd rather not see.

THE NEXT AFTERNOON, Audrey regretted her words as she was met at her house with the sour, hungry faces of several women, all dour-faced, their eyes either lit up with sadistic glee or resignation. A few sported round, pregnant bellies, and the reminder of Audrey's potential to bear a child filled her with horror. She wished with all her might that in the sea of unfamiliar faces she might see Verna, but it was foolish to consider. Verna couldn't be seen here; she had no welcome with the Council wives. Audrey wondered if Verna knew this would happen, and why she didn't warn her. Audrey was particular about her body. She didn't like strangers touching it or looking at it. It made her uncomfortable.

She thought back to the first time she had realized her body was changing. It was her mother who had noticed it first. Audrey remembered how her mother had taken her out for ice cream, and they'd talked about the need to start being careful around boys, and how she might have to start birth control if she wanted to be sexually active. When Audrey had revealed to her mother that she thought she might like women and not boys, Audrey's mother had reacted so glowingly and lovingly, and said she loved Audrey—that it was up to Audrey who she wanted to date. Audrey's eyes teared up at the memory of her mother, who had greeted Audrey in the mornings with such tenderness and adoration; it was sharply unlike the weird, resentful faces that stared down at her now like they wanted to tear her apart.

Audrey cried, tears pouring from her eyes, as she retreated from the women until her back was pressed up against a corner.

"Oh come on, come willingly," Lisbeth said as she forced her way to the front of the Council Wives. "Don't be a baby about it. Unless you have something to hide. Is that it?"

The Council wives murmured, a spontaneous wave of excited gossip. Oh how they would love if Audrey had something to hide.

"I have nothing to hide! Get away from me!"

Audrey held her arms over her chest. Even though she was clothed, she felt naked under their watchful stares.

"No one escapes the Inspection," a young wife tsked.

"Not if you want to become a Council Wife," a gray-streaked crone added.

They all closed in on Audrey—an aggressive, unwanted horde she couldn't repel. She lowered to a crouch in the corner, futilely attempting a shield from their grasp with her hands above her. Audrey was sorely outnumbered. The women tore at her clothes and ripped them off in violent pulls. By the time she was fully naked, she was screaming; her howls were the last attempt at defense—at protest. Lisbeth thwacked her hard across her tear-soaked cheek with three sharp strikes.

The screaming stopped.

"Stop that crying and do as I say," Lisbeth commanded.

When they were done with her, they had concluded that Audrey was pure. She was fit to be married to Councilman Hillard and to become his eighth wife. As she sat crouched in the corner, trying to forget, the Council Wives retreated out of the Callum house, tittering judgmentally about the size of Audrey's hips and breasts, commenting on their thoughts of every last inch of her in a way that made her want to curl into a ball and die.

The worst part was, there was no running water in the house. There was only one common bathing area in the settlement, and she didn't want to be seen washing between her legs there. She would give anything for running water, and a functioning bathtub, so she could scrub out the memory of their old lady hands prying her apart. Lisbeth had taken a special joy in the process, gleefully telling Audrey not to squirm or it would make it worse.

Audrey could never tell Verna about this. It was too painful—too mortifying.

She resolved herself to never speak on it again.

Danny entered the house, a sad look in his eyes.

"I tried to get them to stop, but Dad held me back."

"It's okay," Audrey lied.

Danny searched around for clothes and threw a dress at Audrey. She turned her back to him and put it on. Though she was glad to have any covering at all, she would've felt better in pants and a shirt. She suddenly felt vulnerable in a dress, all too aware of the bareness between her legs. The realization of all that had happened and would happen to her body hit her in a wave of nausea. She doubled over and threw up the bare bits of corn and vegetation they'd eaten in the last few days.

Danny knelt beside her with an old towel and tried to help her clean it up.

"Oh I'm so sorry Audrey," he said over and over again as he cleaned. When he was finished with the floor, he took her in his arms and let her cry.

"I promise it will be okay in the end," he said, and though she wanted to believe him, she wasn't sure that anything would be okay ever again.

Danny carried Audrey to their only cot, which made from old discarded fabrics, strawgrass, and palm. He laid her down on it and offered to bring her fresh water. She agreed, even though she didn't want to be an inconvenience.

When he returned, he sat next to her and nursed her

with the cup, bringing it to her lips to sip as though she were a child or very ill.

"So what do you like about Verna, huh?" He asked, clearly trying to bring a smile to her face.

"She's...wild," Audrey said with a laugh.

"She seems to really like you, Audrey."

"She does." Audrey felt her cheeks flush at the thought.

"How do you think you're going to manage still seeing her once you're married to that asshole?"

"I don't know. We haven't figured that part out yet."

"I don't like this place. I don't think we should've come here."

"There was nowhere else to go. Dad did his best. It's not like we can uproot and travel again. Even if we wanted to, which direction? This was it. There's food here, sunlight, water."

Danny gave her another sip of water. Looking at his eyes, it was evident he had been through immense pain—they had both suffered one trauma after another since Mom died.

"It's not that. It's you. I don't like how they treat women here. You shouldn't have to marry that bastard just to avoid their strange ritual. I don't know how Dad can bear it, frankly."

"Danny. You know he's not the same since Mom..."

"This has nothing to do with Mom."

Danny disliked any mention of their mother, especially as it related to their father's changed demeanor toward them. It wasn't that their father was different entirely, but he had lost part of himself when Isabelle had died in the school bombing. Their father now was more resigned to the world. Whereas he used to fight for even minor injustices, he now thought the best way to survive was to just get along to go along. It wasn't a quality that his children appreciated, but there was no fixing it.

"I'll be fine."

"You should be in college, or starting your first career. Instead you're going to marry the crypt keeper. Yeah, totally fine."

Audrey laughed so hard, tears sprang to her eyes. "The crypt keeper? Jesus Danny, he's not that bad, is he."

Danny nodded in an exaggerated motion. "Oh yeah. He's that bad."

"Don't rub it in."

"I'm just glad to see you laughing."

Danny reached for Audrey's hand and held it in his for a few long moments. He then took her cup and left her in bed to get some rest.

THE SETTLEMENTS WERE abuzz with activity in the week leading up to the Maiden's Feast. Both newer refugees and established residents came together to make something for the preparations. Since they were sacrificing a maiden to Elogona, everyone else likewise had to create or offer something as sacrifice for the feast's eve. Of course, no one sacrificed as much as the maiden. Most of the residents' sacrifices were offerings of food, or light, or music and dance. People prepared art and food according to their ability and desire.

Even though Verna was the planned Maiden, she was still exiled to the settlement's farthest reaches and barely came around the rows of houses during the feast preparations.

Though Audrey wanted to see Verna—and was consumed with thoughts of her—the Council Wives kept Audrey continually in their sight. She was kept busy with a dress-fitting for the feast. The Council Wives got all the first picks of scrap cloth on the island. They had enough to make Audrey a fitted dress just like their own drab garb, and though Audrey said she was fine with what she had, they insisted on making it for her. After they had assaulted her, they took her in as though she were one of them, and it sickened her all the more, this closeness post trauma that they forced on her. She wanted to shove them all off the northern cliffs and watch the Mervosa pick their bones.

There was only one Council Wife who was genuinely kind to Audrey and it was an older woman named Shannon. She had looked away when they had assaulted Audrey, and Audrey had made a note to remember. It had been a deliberate aversion, as though Shannon were abstaining from the whole procedure.

Shannon was Councilman Allen's third wife, and she drew Audrey near to her whenever they were out working or fussing about something as a group.

"It's not so bad," Shannon told Audrey, "There are worse fates nowadays."

Shannon, like most on the island, was resigned to her postwar life. Any hope of change had been meticulously beaten out of her.

"Do you know much about the original Kensington Thirteen?" Audrey asked her one afternoon.

"Oh they don't talk too much about it except when someone starts to question the Feast."

"People question the Feast?"

"Every once in a while, people question the Feast, and then lo and behold, certain folks show up dead..."

"Elogona."

"Maybe."

Shannon gave Audrey a wry smile that suggested something unspoken.

"Hillard."

"Or one of his followers. But it all gets blamed on Elogona besides."

"Why doesn't anyone stop them?"

"Why didn't anyone stop the end of the world, Audrey? Why doesn't anyone stop anyone from hurting one another?" And then, more pointedly, Shannon asked, "Why didn't I stop them from hurting you?"

Audrey thought about it, but had no answer. She didn't like Shannon bringing up the assault because it made her dislike Shannon, and she wanted to like her. It had been over a week since Audrey had been able to interact with Verna—the most she'd been able to do was look at Verna in passing before the Council Wives swept

Audrey away with some mindless feast preparation. She needed a friend, and Shannon was the closest thing to that. Shannon's question made Audrey doubt her own instincts to make Shannon a friend; it made her feel sad and lonelier than ever before.

"If you stopped them, you might've been hurt," Audrey finally offered.

"So there you have it. We're all a little selfish, aren't we?"

Audrey nodded, and they continued on their walk. They searched for coconuts, but spent more time chatting and enjoying the breeze coming in off the ocean. Shannon had been on the island for a while and offered a lot of knowledge to Audrey.

"So is it true, what they say about you?" Shannon asked.

"What?"

"That you like women?"

Audrey blushed. The most she'd ever been with a woman was with Verna, and they'd only kissed and held each other. Verna had never even ventured to touch Audrey in the way that hag Lisbeth had. Verna was sweet, caring—protective, and kind.

Audrey, lost in wishing to see Verna again, realized Shannon was staring at her.

Before Audrey could answer, Shannon leaned in to kiss Audrey.

Audrey backed away, leaving Shannon in the lurch.

The air was awkward and tense between them, a wall that had suddenly sprung up out of nowhere.

"I was just testing you," Shannon lied, and Audrey, not knowing what to say or do, could only nod and continue on walking, looking for stray coconuts.

"You know, I wouldn't tell... I mean, I'd appreciate it if you didn't..."

"I won't tell anyone," Audrey quickly said, and she suddenly wished that she were alone. It felt funny to have longed the moment previous for a friend, but she had sensed something was off with Shannon—for instance, why did the woman want to spend so much time with her when they were doing chores and preparations? Now Audrey knew why. Shannon was attracted to her, or curious. Or lonely. Who knows.

"I shouldn't have done that," Shannon said.

They reached a trail that the Council had made, its borders dotted with large rocks people often used as makeshift chairs. Shannon, visibly distressed, took a seat on one. She ran her fingers through her gray-streaked red hair like she was searching for tangles.

"It's okay," Audrey said, surprising herself. She felt pity for Shannon, who was a lonely woman in just as much of a need for a friend as Audrey.

"It's not okay," Shannon protested. "I'm struggling. I don't even know if I'm attracted to you to be honest—I just, I... I needed to feel something again. Anything. Even if it meant shame. Rejection. Just something. I guess I'm feeling it now."

Audrey took a seat on a nearby rock and contemplated Shannon's words. What was it to lose so much of your life that you would do anything just to feel something again? Is that what being a Council Wife did to you? Did it numb you so much that you flailed and flung yourself at the nearest person just to get a drop of embarrassment—anything to distract yourself from the humdrum, authoritarian existence?

"It's really ok. I'm not scared of you like I am of Lisbeth. Or Hillard."

"Both shit-heels, the lot of them."

Audrey laughed at Shannon's choice of curses.

"I wish someone would just get rid of them," Audrey confessed.

"You're not the only one." Shannon looked around her as she spoke, to make sure no one was listening.

"Do you ever think about getting away from here?" Audrey asked.

"All the time. They say there's nowhere else to go, but I don't believe them. But what can you do? Elogona's out there, and they'd notice a missing fishing boat. Plus, I don't want to go back to the mainland. The disease? The fires? It was terrible."

"I know. I lost my mother in one of the early strikes."

"I lost more than my mother," Shannon said, and before she could say more, Lisbeth appeared, a trail of drably dressed Council Wives following closely behind her.

"Well did you find anything?" Lisbeth spat. All the women behind her carried baskets and bags—but not Lisbeth. She got to relax as she walked, like she was queen of the island.

"Not yet—still scavenging," Shannon said.

"Less talking, more foraging."

Shannon and Audrey nodded without protest. It was important to appear obedient in order to survive. The two women set off down the southern treeline to look for anything to offer up and share at the feast eve celebration. Pickings were slim, now more than ever. Every inch of the island, with exception to the northern cliffs, was picked clean by others. Everyone was looking for that special bit of debris or rare fruit to bring to the celebration. More than that, many wanted to find something precious to offer the Council. Though Audrey couldn't imagine why. She hated those old men.

"What did you do before you came here?"

Shannon took a look around her. She was checking to make sure Lisbeth and the Council Wives weren't around anymore. Audrey found herself doing the same. To be on the island was to constantly be vigilant, Audrey had realized. She was always looking over her shoulder in a way that she hadn't had to do on the mainland, even after the war.

"You'll laugh if I tell you," Shannon said finally, when she was at last certain that they were safe to chat again.

"I won't laugh," Audrey promised.

"I was a hairstylist." Shannon ruffled her gray-streaked, messy hair and both women laughed.

"Do you miss it?"

"Oh I miss a lot of things, but I'm not so sure I miss styling hair. A lot of the customers were...well, let's say they were as pleasant as Lisbeth." Shannon crinkled her nose as if she'd smelled something rotten.

Audrey laughed, but not without first swiveling her head around nervously to make sure it was okay to laugh.

"Oh look here," Shannon said.

She stooped down next to the base of the tree. Audrey got closer to see what Shannon was looking at. It was a baby turtle.

"Should we take him to Lisbeth?" Shannon asked.

"No." Audrey put a hand on Shannon's shoulder and they both met each other's gazes.

"You're right. Let's let him be free a little while longer."

The two women watched the turtle slowly make its way under an upturned root. Audrey bent down and fluffed up some loose foliage around the openings on either side to try to camouflage it better.

"Poor guy doesn't stand a chance, does he?" Audrey said quietly.

She knew if the turtle was found, it would be killed and eaten for the little meat it had under its shell. Audrey understood that this was a necessity for many here, but something about the turtle's vulnerability made her want to protect it, if even for just a little while longer. She wouldn't be able to help if someone else found it during scavenging, but she could try her best to hide it.

"We can't tell Lisbeth we found it," Shannon cautioned.

"Of course not."

"Well we've got to come back with something. We can't have empty hands."

Audrey looked around. There was really nothing in sight that looked like it would please Lisbeth or the Council, or that was even worth sharing.

"We could collect shells?" Audrey offered feebly.

"We could. Some of the women like to braid them in their hair. I suppose it's better than nothing. Food would be ideal."

Audrey knew Shannon was right. Life on the island was always consumed with thoughts of food—when they would get it, where they would get it, how they would preserve it. Much of what they grew here didn't look healthy to Audrey. The vegetables and roots were often misshapen and discolored, as if grown from poisoned soil. Nonetheless, it was all they had to eat, and Audrey found herself ravenously eating gray-speckled long beans and sickly squash when she was hungry enough.

Even the fish that the Council's fishermen brought in often seemed unnatural. Many times the piles they'd bring in with their nets would be full of fish plagued with open sores and veiny eyes. The women scaled the fish and carved out the sores and rot with their knives before boiling them.

Audrey learned that Lisbeth, especially, loved to eat the veiny fish eyes. Lisbeth considered them a delicacy rich in vitamins, and made the other women hand theirs over to her. Audrey had seen the old ghoul pop them into her mouth whole and loll them about over her tongue, from cheek to cheek like a gumball.

The thought was enough to make Audrey ill.

Shannon gathered debris and seashells in her basket. Audrey was sure that another woman would argue to take the turtle back to Lisbeth, but Audrey saw something softer in Shannon's demeanor—something Shannon was used to suppressing for survival.

They walked the shoreline looking for anything that would be considered a treasure, until finally the sun began to set and it was time to return with their meager bounty.

IT WAS the night before Maiden's Feast.

It had been weeks since Verna had been able to meaningfully interact with Audrey. The wretched Council Wives kept her busy with meaningless tasks and feast preparations, so much so that it was impossible to get Audrey alone. The best they could do was exchange long glances as they passed each other in the street and even then, Verna wasn't able to spend too much time walking near the settlement or she was reported to the Council and questioned as to why she was spending so much time there. It was a darkly funny thought that even though Verna was going to be sent to Elogona to keep all their bellies fed, the people still didn't want to have to interact with her.

Danny was different. He sought out Verna at night

for chats, and to let her know that his sister was doing alright. He cried one night as he told her that he was scared for his sister. He recounted how the Council Wives had committed the Inspection, and how Audrey shook afterwards for days—how she looked less like Audrey sometimes and more like a walking ghost.

The stories enraged Verna. She was resentful that she couldn't do more to help. But she expected it. She had seen this same ritual and process many times before with other maidens. It hadn't always been this way—it hadn't always been so punitive and harsh, but the longer they all stayed on the island, the more rules and rituals the Eloganites and Christians imposed.

Since tonight was the eve before Maiden's Feast, all would go out to the southern beaches, close enough to where Verna lived, and sing to Elogona. They'd light fires with palm shavings and old beachwood, and sing sad songs into the late evening. Usually, the maidens were invited to this elegiac celebration before the feast day, and it would be the perfect time to pull Hillard aside.

Ever since her and Audrey's encounter with the ancient Mervosa, Verna had a lot of time to think about how she was going to get Hillard down to the cave. There were memories from her early days on the island, and how Hillard had savagely tried to make her his own—had tried to 'convert' her as he put it, even recruiting the other men to try to assist him in his effort. Verna had fought back, though, and she knew Hillard still sported the scar near his ribcage that she had given him as reward for his sinister plots against her. He had gotten Lisbeth, the wretch, and his other wives to sew him up without much fanfare, but Verna was exiled soon after. He didn't dare admit to anyone on the island what he had tried against her because it was against their law to attempt to sleep with a woman you were not married to, most especially a maiden, but oh how he ensured that Verna would pay for it regardless.

Verna knew the way to get Hillard down to the cave. She would deceive him into thinking she would give him what he tried to take all those years ago, and he would believe her because tomorrow was the feast day, and he'd think she was trying to bribe her way out of it. *Desperate.* She knew how to act desperate.

Verna slipped down to the ocean's edge and tried to scrub some of the dirt off. She splashed saltwater in her face and it stung at her eyes, even after she wiped them clear with the collar of her shirt. She took a comb to her short shaggy hair and brushed the tangles out. A small vial of perfume—a castaway from the mainland that had floated ashore months ago—was finally put to use. She spritzed the stale strawberry aroma all over herself and waited for the first sign of the maiden feast eve celebration. Verna had a clear view down the beachline and could see when the first of the townsfolk appeared, some with makeshift lanterns in hand, others with baskets of mottled food. It wasn't long before sorrowful hymns drifted over the air. For a moment, as Verna watched from a distance, her hair blowing in the warm beach breeze, she thought it looked beautiful. It was a parade of life so far from smoldering devastation. Even as ash and debris floated like snowflakes from across the ocean, there was still song and food.

She took a deep breath and started down the beach at a casual pace. She wanted to give them some time to settle in. She knew a potent sugarcane rum would be passed around, a rarity saved for special occasions as it was incredibly time-intensive to make and not at all important for survival and sustenance of life on the island. And she knew the Council liked to partake in this sugarcane rum—what they called 'fish belly juice' collo-quially—most especially, often asserting their authority to take first drinks of it, and to drink it longer and more than the other townsfolk got to. They also had access to the special cache, which they allowed themselves to take from whenever it was their desire, withholding it from the other townspeople even in times of medical emer-gency when it could serve as a sufficient analgesic.

The celebrations were only beginning when Verna arrived, but most of the townspeople were present. Some were singing at the edge of the ocean, and others tended to lurk a distance away from the water's edge. There were those who were afraid that Elogona's reach could extend to the beach, and they preferred to stay back, keeping their children from the edge. There were women and men assigned to make sure the littlest ones didn't dare go near the water, but it wasn't too much of a problem since most young children on the island were instructed since birth to never go into the ocean.

Eloganite children held the ocean as sacred, and viewed it with respect and fearful awe. The Christian survivor children eyed the water in terror; for them, it was a version of Hell on earth, a place they never wanted to go but feared they'd be sent to if they did or said the wrong thing. For them, Elogona was both boogeyman and devil, and their parents used it to great leverage to control them through use of warning that if they didn't do as they were told, they'd be sent off to Elogona's belly. Verna didn't have children and so she couldn't judge too much on what mothers and fathers did to keep their children obedient, but she felt that life on the island was without a certain joy for children. They grew up in one mode of thought without alternative—without choice. It was why, in part, new mainland arrivals were viewed with suspicion until they assimilated. The existing parents here didn't want their children to be tempted by alternative ways of life, even as the world burned in the distance all around them. They were building a new world, and it was too much like the old. Too restrictive and hateful, full of scorn and judgment. Fire and brimstone. Even as they were surrounded by fire and brimstone, it was still somehow held above their heads as a threat of what was to come. How could it be a threat if it was already here, Verna wondered.

Councilman Hillard nursed a cup of fish belly juice, as did his fellow Councilmen. They sat in a semicircle on chairs. Their wives sat in a huddle, their dress skirts splayed out, on the sand a distance behind them, far away from the ocean's edge, and illuminated by the moonlight and the flame of a few palm lanterns.

Verna saw Audrey's fair face in the flickering lantern

light, and for a brief moment, she smiled. It was so good to see Audrey, especially now that their plan was about to unfold. It felt more hopeful. The air was ripe with possibilities. For once, Verna thought she might be able to be happy. That there was hope. That there was something different than the desolate, dead-end existence of this flat floating rock in the ocean.

Verna worried, though, and she knew that if she could get close enough to speak to Audrey—something she wouldn't dare do here in front of everyone—that Audrey would tell her the same thing. They didn't know much about the Mervosa. It could be a trick. The only thing that made Verna feel slightly more comfortable was that the Mervosa didn't think she tasted good. It didn't mean that the Mervosa wouldn't kill her, but Verna at least felt certain that the Mervosa wouldn't *eat* her. Unless, of course, she proved tastier than Councilman Hillard—a distinct possibility.

Sand gnats swarmed around her head and nibbled at her neck. They probably liked the strawberry spritz that she had put on. It was odd—the things that washed ashore sometimes. All manner of personal artifacts, sometimes even whole water-logged couches or old appliances. They usually had to find ways to dispose of the unusable items —generally a contained pit fire, but there were other times the items proved useful. Clothes that could be dried out in the sun. Dishes that could be boiled and re-used. Sometimes items, like the strawberry perfume, were a small luxury, a small token of memory from the past. It was difficult for Verna to remember her life before arriving at the island, but those small items sometimes brought back memories of a different time, when she had imagined a future very much unlike the one she was living now.

There was still hope, though. She could get some semblance of that future back. The future where she imagined herself as a doctor—the thought made her laugh now—or a scientist, living comfortably in a city condo with her girlfriend. Girlfriend—also a joke of a dream until she met Audrey, of course. Audrey.

Verna had to get to Councilman Hillard and convince him to go off with her. It would be hard to do because of all the eyes on her as she moved through the crowd.

"Praise you," Carol Jennings said to Verna as she walked past. Carol was an Eloganite acolyte. She had a small lantern in her hand and a feverish expression, as if she wanted to bow to Verna, kiss her feet, or absorb into her. Fanatic reverence always scared Verna. It led to bad things.

Once Carol Jennings was heard saying "Praise you," the rest of the Eloganites followed suit. "Bless you!" and "Praise you!" they hailed, even as others continued their mournful song. Some small groups set out on the sand with small baskets and ate bits of fruits, nuts, and fish until Elogona matched their own song with its elegiac wailing.

"It's Elogona!" a child exclaimed, full of excitement and awe.

"Yes, it's coming to eat you," another said, and made wiggly hand motions.

A mother swatted at the children, wagging a finger at them to stop.

There was the sound of insects, and flickering flame, the smell of people gathered together, of sweat and ripe fruit. Verna had one mission—to take the Councilman Hillard far from here, to the northern reach of the island, to a place where others wouldn't go looking for them. She would feed him to the carapaced witch who had escaped Elogona to her lonely cave, living for all eternity now as nothing more than rumor. The witch's history was only known to the witch—she was the last of her kind—and no one would be able to remember her in the way Verna's mother would remember her daughter. What was it like to be the last of your kind? Verna knew what it was like to be one of a kind, but she still had the feeling that there were more out there like her, and that she only had to meet them. Verna didn't subscribe to the belief that they were a last paradisiacal bastion for humanity. Verna was certain there were more settlements out there—*better* settlements. Humans had to amount to more than this cultish rendering.

Verna finally neared Councilman Hillard. Councilman Tompkins looked up at her, his lips unmoving but a smile in his eyes.

Hillard barely looked at her at first, too busy taking in all who gathered on the beach—a king overseeing the court. She leaned in close to him, so close that she could smell the sugar rum on his breath.

"Let's finish what you started so long ago," she whispered in his ear, and she let herself flick her tongue surreptitiously at his earlobe. It pained her to do it, but it was in service of letting him know what was on offer—in service of luring him to his death. He would pay for what he had done to these people.

Hillard looked up, his expression inscrutable. Verna worried he would reject her offer, or that he'd lambast her in front of everyone. If her plan failed, all would be lost, as there would be no other way to get him to the northside cliffs.

Instead, he smiled a sickly smile, and murmured something indecipherable into Tompkins's ear. Tompkins laughed and took in Verna with his eyes in a way that made her insides churn. She truly hoped Tompkins wouldn't come along because that would complicate matters. She wasn't sure of the extent of the Mervosa's powers, and she worried that the witch wouldn't be able to handle two men at the same time.

Instead, Tompkins remained behind as Hillard got up. She followed behind Hillard, the scent of rum wafting through the air to her nose.

In the background, the hymns of the Eloganites became softer and fainter as they walked on. When Verna realized that he was taking her toward the settlement, she called out to him, "Wait!"

He turned around and stepped closer to her. "You want me here? In the wild, like an animal?"

He reached a hand for the edge of her shirt, and she jumped at the touch of his leathery fingers. They were clammy and old, like something that had crawled up from the grave. She had fended him off before, but what if she couldn't do it again? What if she couldn't get him to go to the northside with her, and to the cave? Worse, what if he knew about the Mervosa? Maybe he knew, and that's why he had stifled rumors for so long.

"Not here," she said, as sweetly as she could.

"My house," he suggested, and grabbed her hand in his. His thumb stroked her hand with an earnestness that made her want to vomit.

"No, not there either. I don't want anyone to know."

"Well where then?"

His hand in hers, she led him away from the main trail and toward the northside.

"The cliffs? I'm too tired for all that," he called out. He laughed a little—a strange drunken giggle that fell from his lips into the night-air—a mixture of rum and sex and glee.

She led him onward despite his protests. Soon Verna realized that the old man would follow her to the ends of the earth to get inside of her. As they walked, she heard him stumbling back and forth. There was temptation to shove him off the cliffs and let him fall to his death, rather than having to climb down with him to the Mervosa's lair. Shoving him seemed risky, though. He might live and she wasn't sure if she was strong enough to fight him if she wasn't able to get him off the cliffs in one push. Plus the paths down the cliffs were scattered enough that it wasn't likely he'd die unless she shoved him so hard he flung outward by a good length, and Verna was positive she didn't have that kind of physical strength. She wasn't sure any human had that kind of strength.

No, it was better to stick to the original plan and get him to the cave. The Mervosa was waiting with her green globular light, skittering on the walls with her many legs and sniffing for fish, no doubt. A sea witch—the last of her kind. Could Verna trust a deal with a sea witch? She knew so little about the ancient beasts of this world. The time of humans was long past, and she felt ill-prepared for it, like a mite in a terrarium, so small and weak as to be meaningless. Still, although she was small and weak, she had a mission. For her. For Audrey. For all that could have been and might still be.

The songs from the south side of the island faded to a distant mournful murmuring. An elegiac hum lingered in the background as they walked farther and farther north. The terrain became more tumultuous and unpredictable. Hillard jammed his foot against a boulder and let out a yelp. The harder the walk became, the more his giddiness subsided. Verna began to sense a power shift; she was becoming less prey and more predator. And he—he was far more vulnerable away from his followers—away from all those who enabled a man like Hillard to stay in power. She wondered what would happen if those followers could see the flash of fear in his eyes in the moonlight. Would they still follow him then? Would they still fear him and bend knee? Would they still let him take their daughters as wives, swishing fish belly juice in his mouth while he spouted off why they had to sacrifice maidens to the creature in the sea?

Hillard was one of the Kensington Thirteen, one of the original people to settle on this island. He often talked about how he had the foresight to settle here before the world went to ash, and now was no different. He started recollecting and speaking on the matter as though it gave him a boost of confidence.

"I've always had a bit of the prophesying about me. I knew you'd come around," he said.

Verna smiled because they had finally reached the cliffs. He reached for her with his leathery hand, and slid his thick, mole-crusted fingers up her tunic. She emitted a fake moan, and then said in a soft whisper, "Not here, down there. In the cave."

She pointed over the edge of the cliff. The path was obscured in the nighttime, the moonlight playing tricks across the mixed foliage, sand and rock, the ocean waves musically lapping at the cliffs. Hillard uneasily walked closer to the cliff path and looked over the edge. She thought she saw him shudder as he looked. He was scared. Uneasy. Was he too scared? Was his arousal greater than his fear, or was his fear greater than his arousal? Tomorrow was the Maiden's Feast and if he didn't take her now, he would lose his chance. Verna was sure this is what spurred him to take the first foothold down the path. When he looked up at her as he descended, his expression looked both lustful and threatening.

"You'd better be worth it, girl. I don't want to hear a single no out of your mouth when we get down there."

Verna was relieved, watching him climb down the

path. He was steadier-footed than she would've expected, but it might've been the higher stakes and steep terrain that sobered him up. She'd seen drunker men than Hillard sober up in such situations, but it didn't mean the alcohol wasn't still taking hold in his body, numbing his sharpness of thought.

Verna followed him, leaving a space between his arms and her legs so that he couldn't pull her if he lost his balance. She didn't want to go down with him if he fell. It was hard to not think of Audrey as they descended the cliff. It had been so long since she'd felt Audrey's blonde tendrils in her hand—so long since she had run her lips over Audrey's sun-kissed skin. Even if things went badly tonight, even if somehow Verna ended up not returning to the southern settlements, she knew Audrey would be better off without Hillard. She knew the world would be better off without Hillard.

If good people didn't rid the world of bad men, who would? Most people stepped aside and let the loudest voices rule, so long as those loud voices persecuted someone else. For most, it was easy to sit back and let *other people* suffer. Verna could never be like that—she knew what it was like to be othered. And when she saw something was wrong in the world, she wanted to make it right.

"Hap-py," she said softly to the rock-face, and the thought of her mother and father, and the home they once shared together on the mainland, the jobs her parents went to, the cars they rode in, and the silly everyday activities that had occupied all their waking thoughts—it all came crashing down in Verna's mind as she finished descending onto the sand. Hillard was there waiting for her when her feet landed. He stared, transfixed, at the reverse U-shaped cave.

"I've never seen this place before," he said, surprised.

"It's often covered by the high tide. We're lucky the tide is out right now."

"Well we better be quick about it then. You first."

Verna entered the cave without hesitation, but she didn't like having her back to Hillard. Fear swallowed her thoughts and memories as she walked inside. She was scared of Hillard, and scared of the Mervosa, but more so, she was fearful that the Mervosa somehow wouldn't be there. That the sea witch had lied, and that Verna would have to claw and fight Hillard with her bare hands. If she could even fight just long enough for the high tide to come in and take them both away to Elogona, then it was worth it. What was a day early to feed a beast, anyway?

If the plan didn't work, there would be no point in living.

The tide was out, but it would be coming back soon enough. The cave was much darker inside at night. When Audrey and Verna had gone together, their eyes were able to adjust in the dark in the antechamber so that they could see the rock formation outlines. Now, in the darkness of night, Hillard and Verna couldn't see anything. It was pitch black.

"Where are you?" Hillard called for her. She realized he couldn't see her at all, and she couldn't see him. She took one step away from his voice, careful not to fall on the jagged rock floor.

A hand grasped at her—it was Hillard's groping fingers in the dark. They dragged at her tunic and tried to pull her closer. Verna screamed as loudly and shrilly as she could. Hillard's fist reached out and made contact with her face, but she had leaned back in time as he swung so that the impact was lessened. Verna stumbled backwards in the dark.

Where was the Mervosa...

She didn't have an alternate plan. There wasn't a back-up plan other than fighting for her life against the man who had made her existence hell on earth. The man who had torn her parents from her. The man who had sent her to exile because he wasn't able to have his way with her. That fucking bastard, she thought.

Suddenly Verna decided she didn't need the Mervosa after all. She'd get started on Hillard herself.

Verna lunged in the dark toward Hillard. She leapt on him with the full force of her body and they both went lurching, moving deeper into the cave as they fell, both swinging blindly and sometimes landing blows. He grabbed a section of her hair and beat her head against the wall. Fingers groped at her shirt, and when an arm brushed against her face, she pulled it closer and bit so deeply she drew the iron tang of blood.

Hillard howled and wrenched his arm free from Verna's teeth.

Maybe it was the scent of the blood that drew out the sea witch, or maybe it was the sound of the scuffle. Or maybe, as Verna suspected, maybe it had been watching all the while and was waiting to see how things would shake out between this man and Verna.

The green globule bounced from outside the tunnel and behind it came skittering the witch on her many legs. Its lips looked scary as ever, their form so small but Verna knew better. She knew the muscular tapeworm of a tongue that came out from that deceptive opening.

Hillard looked worse for wear in the green light. He stood, as though he couldn't believe his eyes, and stared at the monstrous Mervosa before him.

"They warned me about you!" He cried out.

"Nothing to be afraid of, little Tasty," the Mervosa soothed. "We're just going to have a bit of a chomp."

Hillard swung his fist at one of the Mervosa's many eyes and it skittered backwards before angling its arthropodic body upwards on four back legs. "Silly man," the witch scolded.

Hillard broke his spell of terror and in what he surely knew would be his last moments, he turned to Verna with intense hatred in his eyes, anger and defeat emanating off of him in the globule's green light. "You bitch. You led me here to die."

Hillard took a last lurch toward Verna, but the Mervosa was quicker than his human form. Its tongue, thick and meaty, extended out from the witch's uncanny maw and looped its spindly muscle around Hillard's head. The tongue muffled his screams and picked him up, flailing him back and forth until his neck snapped with a decisive pop. Then, in a sight Verna longed to look away from but couldn't—the horror was too acute—Verna watched the sea witch lap at Hillard with its tongue, leaving his fresh corpse coated in a frothy white saliva.

"It softens the meat," the Mervosa said.

Verna longed to leave the cave and return to the southern side of the island where people lived, close to Audrey. But the Mervosa and Hillard's corpse were between Verna and the cave's exit.

"You brought me a tasty meal. I will enjoy it," the Mervosa said, tongue safely back behind the sneaky wall of its lips.

"You can do something for me in return," Verna said softly. She was going out on a limb, but she had to take the chance.

"What more do you want from me?"

Verna told the Mervosa how she loved Audrey, how they wanted to escape this place before the Feast, and how they couldn't love each other here safely. Verna was truly surprised at how much she confessed to the sea witch, and she hoped she wouldn't regret it.

When Verna was done revealing all to the Mervosa, except the lie they told about Elogona, the Mervosa extended its tongue toward Verna and touched its spiked tip to her forehead again, this time drawing a drop of blood which it quickly lapped up.

"Less sweet this time. You have a taste that reminds me of an old place," the Mervosa remarked. Verna wanted out of the cave so badly, she could feel it in her bones, but at the same time, she was desperate for the sea witch to help in some way, or to provide guidance.

"You taste like the old Hills of Xh'Xh'Loui'xx. Back when I was young, newly formed from the cursed flame of those before me. There was a tenderness in those hills. It was in the soil." The sea witch kneaded Hillard's corpse with its many legs, "but tenderness will get you killed. You have to eat or be eaten."

"I see you cannot help me," Verna concluded sadly. "Then I should be getting back."

The sea witch grabbed the bouncing green globule of light, and in the sea witch's front two legs, the light went dim and hard like a rock. "This is the last of its kind," the Mervosa said. "The last of its kind from the last of a kind."

The Mervosa extended the globule toward Verna until she took it in her hands. The rock was hot to the touch.

"Smash it open when you need to, but know that when you smash it, it will unleash something you cannot stop. It should be used only as a last resort."

"What will you do without it?"

"I will live in the dark. Until my flame yields another like me. One day." The Mervosa skittered back toward Hillard's corpse. "Now go. I want to be alone with my food."

VERNA FELT her way for the cave entrance and crawled out onto the sand. The moonlight looked awfully bright once she was outside. She kept the globule, now hardened into a geode, in her hands and it warmed her palms. She'd have to be careful holding it as she ascended the cliff path. Her muscles were worn out. She was awfully tired after traveling all this way alone, the adrenaline of what she pulled off finally settling in as exhaustion.

She wanted to get away from the sea witch as soon as possible. She could hear the creature breaking and licking the bones of her meal. Verna brushed the spot on her forehead where the Mervosa had touched her with its spindly tongue. There was a small rough dot, as if it were swelling. The scar of a sea witch's touch. She hoped no one else would ask her about the mark because she didn't have a good excuse ready.

Fortunately, all of that could wait for tomorrow. For tonight, Verna would head back to her own shack and resume her exile. She knew it would be a while yet before anyone was alarmed at Hillard missing, especially with Tompkins covering for him. The real worry was if Tompkins was going to mention that they went off together, or question her about it.

Verna let the moonlight guide her as she scrambled up the cliff path, making sure to hold onto the geode in her hand. It was magically still warm, as if the rock-like exterior were hiding something inside. Verna thought of the striking green light that had filled the cave's antechamber. Perhaps that's what would come out when she smashed it. But how could that be, she wondered?

The Mervosa had said once Verna smashed it, it would be something she unleashed that she couldn't take back. It couldn't be just a light. There had to be some other trick to it. Nonetheless, Verna wasn't about to use it unless absolutely necessary. It was the last trick she had up her sleeve, should she need it. Anything to get her and Audrey to safety. And where *was* safety? Where would they go?

By the time Verna was back on the path headed toward the southern beaches and her shack, she was too tired to come up with any viable plan. She needed sleep if she was going to think clearly.

AUDREY HAD SEEN Verna leave with Hillard, but neither had come back after they'd left. It had taken Audrey all the restraint she had to not follow Verna out to the cliffs, to not stalk behind them like some lioness in the night. But Audrey wasn't able to so much as move without Lisbeth or the other Council Wives leering at her.

Audrey found it despicable how the other women kept her around like she were some possession of Hillard's. Didn't they have any dignity?

She spotted Danny sitting alone on the beach with a makeshift lantern of his own. Had he made it? Danny had begged their father for a workshop of his own back home. He loved to make things with his hands. Even when he was a little boy, he'd take bars of soap that Mom bought for the bath and instead take a knife to them, whittling away. His first figurines weren't too good, but slowly over time he got better and eventually he could make little creatures out of the soap bars. Gnomes and butterflies—cute little carvings that he'd put on her dresser for when she woke up for school. She watched him now, sitting by himself, his heels close to the edge of the ocean tide. The moon was fading and the sun would rise soon. Many of the townsfolk had already gone home to their houses and even half of the Council Wives had left. Lisbeth stayed, though she was half in the can on whatever strange alcohol they had been drinking. She had doled it out to the other wives like a queen granting favors, letting them take small sips here and there. Audrey was never offered a sip and didn't care. She hadn't the stomach for alcohol. Besides, she wanted to keep her mind sharp for when Verna returned.

Verna *must* return. Everything just *had* to be okay.

The other wives distracted, Audrey took a chance to get up and walk toward her brother Danny. "You look so lonely over here."

"I am a little lonely."

"Well I guess no matter where you go, that thing is always out there huh."

"Elogona?"

"Yeah."

Audrey stared out at the ocean, streaked with red from the rising sun on the horizon. It looked like blood streaks, like there had been widespread carnage. She wondered what Elogona looked like.

"Do you ever think back to when we were in Bible class when we were little?"

"Not really."

Audrey playfully kicked Danny. It felt so good to be near her brother. It wasn't until they had lost Mom that Audrey fully realized how important it was to have someone in the world who shared your childhood with you, someone who understood that world you had to experience as you learned the ins and outs of earth—how to walk and see, how to play and create. Someone who was around when you first broke a bone, and when you discovered movies, and when you went on your first road trip. After a parent died, you wanted to go back over every memory and the fewer people there were to do that with, the harder it was. She leaned into Danny and let him put his arm around her. Despite everything, at least they were alive. They had made it. Mom would have wanted it that way.

"I was thinking about Sunday school, about the Bible class, and I remember them telling us about the strange creatures that used to walk the earth before man."

"You don't really believe all that, do you."

Audrey felt the urge to tell him then about what she and Verna had seen in the cave. She wanted to tell him everything about the sea witch, and about the plan to feed Hillard to him—about how he probably was already dead, if everything went well. If it didn't go well—never mind, Audrey wasn't even going to consider that possibility. She would only think positive. It was the early morning of the Maiden's Feast day and she had to think positive because there was no way she could marry that bastard Hillard, and there was no way she wanted to see Verna sacrificed to Elogona.

"I don't know if I believed it then, but I feel more open to it now. They say that the creatures are coming back. Like spiders that hibernate in the ground and suddenly come up when it thaws. What if the age of man is over, Danny? What if we're vestiges?"

Danny smiled at Audrey, "I don't believe in all that, Audrey. I don't believe in any of this," Danny gestured around at the sleepy-eyed celebrants on the beach. "I don't believe in Elogona either."

"Then what makes that noise?"

"Probably some trick the Council made up. Think about it—this tale of Elogona? It gives them all the power. They get to take as many wives as they want, and whenever they dislike someone, they can get rid of them and say Elogona ate them."

Audrey disagreed with her brother, but she also saw inside his soul—the fact that he liked to deal with hammers and nails, soap and knives, tools of the earth, and his very hands—that he couldn't deal with the fact that the earth had changed. Audrey watched the sun continue to rise over the ocean, and as if listening in on their conversation, Elogona's mournful wails rose up from the water and over the beach. Most were used to it by now—they were accustomed to the sound of the impending doom that circled their rock in the sea—day and night, every hour, mourning their eventual demise.

"We're fossils, Danny. We just don't know it yet."

Ash came in on a breeze and flecked Danny's sweat-shirt. He looked down at the gray flakes. Who knows where they had come from—maybe they had even flown all the way from the city Audrey and Danny had once lived in, maybe they were remnants from some bombed-out place...maybe even from the school where Mom had died, Audrey thought bitterly.

Audrey couldn't think of her mother without becoming intensely sad. She knew how her mother died even though she wasn't there. Her mother would have done anything possible to protect the children she was with. Mom wasn't scared like Audrey. Mom had the spirit of a lion. Why did women with the spirits of lions always get taken too soon?

She had to snap out of it. She had to get some gumption.

Mom wouldn't have wanted her to sit on the beach and wallow.

"Seems like they're up to something," Danny said and he nodded over at the group of the Council Wives, who were stirring awake. Many of them circled around Lisbeth who looked frantic and upset. That old hag.

Lisbeth called out to the group of lingering cele-brants, "We can't find our husband. We can't find Coun-cilman Hillard!"

"Have you checked the settlement?" a man in a red

sweater asked. He looked like he had been dozing off when Lisbeth's voice awakened him.

"That's Councilman Allen," Danny whispered.

"Of course we've checked the settlement! What do you think I am—an idiot?" Lisbeth shrilled.

Councilman Allen stumbled to his feet. He met eyes with Councilman Tompkins, who was coming out of the bush and toward the group of townsfolk. Allen met Tompkins's eyes and asked, "You seen him?"

"I saw him last night, he was with that devil's whore. Verna."

"We've got to warn her," Danny whispered.

"Danny, I can't go anywhere. They'll see me. Can you go and tell her?"

Danny leapt to his feet and started running. He was fast, but the men chasing after him were also fast.

Lisbeth came up to where Audrey was sitting—two other wives, Nancy and Rinella—behind her.

"Don't let her leave," Lisbeth instructed.

"I haven't done anything!" Audrey protested.

"I'll be the judge of that," Lisbeth sneered.

The sun cast harsh light on them all.

III

Verna knew there was trouble when she heard her name being screamed. It was Danny. She could recognize his voice by now after all the times he had visited her alone at night to tell her updates about her sweet Audrey. Was he in trouble?

She had not gotten enough sleep. Even though every ounce of her body was exhausted, she couldn't bring herself to fall asleep when she had laid down after the cliffs. She had spent the night thinking about what happened to Hillard, and how perhaps his death was too merciful, a snapped neck instead of something prolonged. He should have suffered, she thought bitterly.

She thought about silly things, too, like if they got out of here, what would be the first thing that she and Audrey did together. What if they found a settlement that was nicer than this one? A place where they could go and set up a home together. It was a foolish thought. Today was the Maiden's Feast day and Verna would be

sent to Elogona. At least she spared Audrey the death of
marriage to Hillard, though. At least she spared her love
that pain. But part of her knew they'd marry Audrey to
another one of the Council, or to another man on the
island. There was no way for women to escape the
oppressive will and sadistic whimsy of men. At least it
wasn't Hillard, but did it really matter if she was just
going to be married off to someone else? Verna wondered
if they'd accomplished anything in bringing Hillard to the
sea witch after all.

It was a cruel joke, and a thought flashed in her
mind, like a backdrop to all the other thoughts—the
image of the sea witch laughing in the darkness. Hadn't it
been their first visit to the witch that had started all of
this?

Of course, she did have the mysterious geode. That
had to be worth something. The Mervosa hadn't
explained how it would work, which was a problem. And
there was no way to test it without using it, and to use it
would mean it was gone and couldn't be stopped, whatever that meant.

"Verna!"

Audrey was snapped out of her puzzled thoughts
when Danny came crashing into her shack. She quickly
hid the geode and pushed him out, following him into the
open air. Danny's panicked breaths, and the urgent way
in which he had burst into her home—she had to steel
herself for whatever was coming. The Council and
several other townsmen were already upon them. They
must have followed Danny closely when he took off

running. Several of them were red in the face, not used to running so fast in the hot sun.

"Is Audrey ok?" she asked Danny quickly in a hushed tone.

"She's fine."

Tompkins reached the two of them, with Allen close behind, and he took Verna roughly by the arm. Danny intervened and wedged himself between them. Verna wanted to tell Danny to stop. She knew they needed Verna to sacrifice to Elogona, but they didn't need Danny. If anything, they'd be all too happy to rid the island of another young man, especially one as good-natured and likable as Audrey's brother. She didn't want Danny to give them an excuse.

"Stop that! Get off her."

Danny shoved Tompkins back, and Tompkins looked at the boy as if he pitied him, as if Danny were an ant that he could squash under his shoe. Verna was terrified for Danny when she saw the sinister gleam in Tompkins's eye. She'd seen the way Tompkins had ripped apart live sea critters before; that man enjoyed playing with his food. Danny wasn't as strong as Tompkins or Allen.

"You like to make things with those hands, yeah?" Allen asked.

"Oh you like to give handjobs, is that it?" Tompkins cracked.

Danny's face turned bright red.

Verna whispered in his ear, "It's okay, Danny. Don't get yourself hurt. I can take care of myself."

"No." Danny said defiantly, not even looking at

Verna. "Somebody's gotta stand up to these guys. Somebody has to tell them they can't go around acting like that!"

Tompkins grabbed Danny and Allen slugged him in the stomach. His sweet eyes met Verna and he mouthed the word *run*.

She darted into the shack, grabbed the geode and ran out the back, her legs pounding the sand as fast as they could. As soon as she saw the bushline, she leapt into it, letting thorns and bristles scrape her skin apart as she sprinted as far away from the southern edge as possible. She'd go north and hide by the rock wall. As she ran, she could hear Danny's cries.

She looked at the geode in her hand.

Audrey never felt so much pain in her life as she did when Tompkins and Allen dragged her brother Danny back by his arms across the beach.

"Hey take a look at Danny boy!" Tompkins yelled out to her.

"Oh Danny Boy..." Allen sang in a mockery.

What they had done to her brother was beyond evil.

"No," she said, the word almost caught in her throat. It was strained and much too soft. She wanted to scream but there was the overwhelming sense that it was pointless to do so. All of her breath and energy hardened into a stone pit in her stomach. She could scarcely get the oxygen to cry out, and for a breathless moment, Audrey worried her heart may have stopped its timid beating.

They had smashed all of Danny's fingers. His two hands were pulverized—they were now dripping and flayed globs of flesh. He'd never make anything again with those hands. Danny slipped in and out of consciousness. She could see that he was losing a lot of blood. The sight was such a shock—even after seeing missile and drone aftermath on the mainland—somehow, the sight of the red, dark blood seeping into the sand under the bright afternoon sun sent Audrey into mental paralysis. She wanted to look away, but couldn't. She wanted to run to her brother, and to hold his bleeding head in her hands, but she couldn't. She wanted, most of all, to watch the entire Council burn, but she hadn't the power to make that happen. A last thought—a desperate thought—occurred to her that she might pray, but then the morbid realization that others' prayers and rituals were the reason she was in this position in the first place made her decide not to. There was no prayer. There was no hope. Only the thought of Verna flashed in her mind. Maybe—*maybe* Verna could survive.

"And the whore?" Lisbeth asked, not even acknowledging Danny with a breath.

"The whore ran off. We'll search for her later. She went to the north side."

"Get the boat ready," Lisbeth ordered.

"It's early," Tompkins cautioned.

There were murmurs from the crowd on the beach.

More people had come out from the settlement to see what was happening. People flocked out from their huts and shacks, some half-dressed, others sleep weary still, and they swarmed the scene like gnats to a carcass. None seemed moved by the sight of her pulverized brother bleeding out on the sand, and for that, Audrey was filled with a rage so hot she wondered if it couldn't burn through anything she touched.

"I'll decide if it's early or not," Lisbeth scowled.

"We don't have Verna, though. We don't have the maiden," Nancy softly said.

"Oh she's not a maiden anymore," Tompkins chuckled.

Lisbeth's cheeks flushed with anger. "What's that supposed to mean?"

Tompkins gave her a glance. "She lured your husband away last night. Seduced him, I'd say. Used her devil's tongue on him."

"I'll say," Allen muttered.

Audrey hated them all. She loathed how they were speaking about Verna, but she loathed them more for the fact that they could joke when her brother was dying right before her eyes. Audrey knew what they didn't know. She knew that Verna had lured Hillard out to the sea witch's cave. It was the sea witch Audrey was more worried about—not Hillard. She hoped Verna had made it out of that dark and lonely cave, tucked away in the cliffs on the north side of the island. She knew Hillard was dangerous, but Audrey feared more the mysterious powers of that strange creature, the Mervosa. Only now,

Audrey wished she were back in the dark recess with the many-legged witch. Being wrapped up in its terrifying and thick tongue would have been preferable to being under the watch of these hypocrites. Oh how she loathed them all. She considered reaching up toward Lisbeth and biting into her throat—any last stand to make the agony end.

Audrey was ready to go. She was ready to leave this place, and to join her mother in the great Nothing that laid beyond. Only, it was Verna that she would miss... brave Verna. Verna, who wasn't afraid to swim with Elogona—Verna, who traveled to the witch's northern cave in the dead of night. Her Verna.

I will wait for you, Audrey thought in a silent message. That message would never reach its destination, she knew, but she urged her thoughts all the same. *I will wait for you, Verna, in the darkness beyond. I'll be the shadow that holds you dear when your time here is over. I'll be...*

Lisbeth's hard stare snapped Audrey out of her reverie. Audrey tried to look away but there was something about the intensity of Lisbeth's gaze that made Audrey compelled to stare back. It was like looking into an abyss.

"Well this one's a maiden. I've verified it myself," Lisbeth remarked, full of self-satisfaction.

Murmurs ran up and down the beach as more and more people gathered. Some of the townsfolk looked confused, and one called out, "Why is there violence on this merry day?" An Eloganite, no doubt.

She could hear side conversations break out amongst the group. People were no doubt trying to gather their bearings and figure out what had happened. It was unusual for a new maiden to be chosen like this. The maiden was decided long before the feast preparations, and once it was chosen, it was considered ill fortune to decide another. It had happened from time to time, but this no doubt seemed strange to the Eloganites and other settlers. Murmurs ran rampant among the crowd, and Audrey wondered if any one of them would stop Lisbeth, but she knew better. Audrey knew people didn't question authority—not in any way that mattered.

Tompkins spoke, weighing their options. "Well let's find another, yeah? She's awfully pretty to send to the Elogona." An old man just like Hillard, Tompkins could only think of himself. Audrey knew he was already plotting the possibility of taking Audrey into his bed, now that Hillard was nowhere to be found. Tompkins doubtlessly saw the Council leader's misfortune as his own blessing. *What outstanding hypocrites*, Audrey sourly thought. She'd rather slit her own throat than have to even speak one word to Tompkins. When she looked at him, all she wanted was to see him destroyed.

"I want her to pay," Lisbeth said through gritted teeth, and she flashed Tompkins such a stare that he shrank back from her wrath.

"Hear me!" Lisbeth called out to the crowd. "We have lived on this island for many years in peace, and we welcome refugees. I daresay we welcome them! But a few who we took in with open arms have betrayed us. And one of them, here, who my husband was gracious enough to ask to couple, has betrayed him! She sent him to his doom! Now, hear me when I say she must pay!"

Lisbeth yelled the words as if she had divine authority. It was bone chilling to hear the confident zeal with which Lisbeth proclaimed, as if she had a badge of moral mastery.

There was an agreeable roar from the crowds on the beach. Lisbeth's proclamations moved the followers to zealous tears and shouts. They rallied around her and surged in a tight circle. Audrey was claustrophobic from their shared hysteria. Alone, a dissenting voice was heard in the distance.

"Danny! Audrey! Where are my children?"

Audrey's father ran from the crowd. Tompkins grabbed him at his waist and her father decked him in the face. Seeing her father fight back made Audrey want to fight, too. Even if just to get a moment to touch him, to hold him—to be held by someone who loved her. She hadn't agreed with a lot of her father's decisions, but she knew he loved her. He loved Danny, too, and had only wanted the best for them. Audrey jumped to her feet and tried to run toward her dad, but she was stopped by the Council Wives, who held her and clawed her back with glee. Unkempt nails scraped across her back as she writhed and wriggled to get out of the womens' hold. Their arms clenched tighter around her until their coordinated grips closed like a vice.

"Don't you hurt my father!" Audrey screamed. As she yelled the words, her ribs pressed against the tight hold of the Council Wives, and it caused her midsection a stinging pain. It was hard to get the breath and energy to press against their grip enough to speak, let alone yell.

"He won't be a father much longer," Lisbeth said quietly. There was evil in her eyes. "One dead on the beach. One dead in the belly."

Audrey looked over to where Danny was left to bleed out on the beach. His chest was no longer moving.

With her father screaming and struggling to reach her, for Audrey the world ended for a second time. Any feeling or desire to fight left her body like a natural bodily evacuation, and Audrey soon became the shell of the person who was once Audrey Callum. The war—this place—these dreadful people—they had taken everything from her, even hope.

I will wait for you. She sent her thought one more time into the great ether of consciousness and hoped that her love, Verna, could catch it on the wind, could dream it one day and know Audrey had thought it in her final moments.

She looked to the sky hoping to see an angel or spirit, any sign of life beyond this one. "I want my mother." She heard herself say the words, but felt outside of her own body, looking down at a girl crying so hard she was thrashing and vomiting.

Who was that girl? Was it her?

They dragged her toward the boat. There was rope now, and it was being tied around her ankles. The rope was thick and it grated against her skin. It was too strong. There was no use in trying to struggle, she thought.

Audrey thought of Verna, of Danny, or her father. She hoped they wouldn't hurt her father more than he was already hurt, but she couldn't see him now. She was laying flat in one of the fishing boats, and now they were tying her wrists together over her chest. Soon a cloaked group of Eloganites surrounded the boat and began chanting, "Go with God, Praise You Maiden," over and over until their chants drowned out the sounds of her father crying for her. She knew he wanted to jump into the boat with her.

She couldn't see much other than the sky and the people who looked over her from the edges of the boat. Soon she could feel the boat was in the air, and her body rocked back and forth in the wooden shell.

Finally, the water took her and they were shoving the boat out, farther and farther into the ocean until the current took it away. She was alone now.

A gift for a god.

VERNA HAD RUN to the cliffs and circled back surreptitiously, where she spied on the group from the bush-line. The hot geode in her hand was warmer than it had been when the Mervosa had first given it to her.

Verna's heart swelled with pain when she saw what they had done to Danny.

Oh Danny, damn you, she thought. She didn't know

why the kid had defended her. Nobody ever defended Verna. It made her feel both affection and anger toward him. Anger because she now felt guilt for causing his death. And then that made her angry, too, because no one should ever deserve what they did to Danny. His hands were inhuman, like ground meat. She couldn't imagine the unbearable pain he had been in, to be beaten like that and then thrown on the sand under the harsh sun. It was cruel and evil.

But that wasn't the main cause of Verna's boiling rage.

The zealous bastards had tied Audrey up and had set her off to sea in one of the fishing boats. They were giving Audrey to Elogona.

Well damn you all to hell, Verna thought. *Damn every last one of you to hell.*

She watched as Lisbeth let the townsfolk carry her on their shoulders. Lisbeth led the chant, "Praise you Maiden! Praise you!" Their chanting echoed throughout the island as Audrey's boat drifted listlessly.

Verna was too angry to cry. She knew Audrey, alone in that boat after watching her brother die, was terrified. And poor Audrey's father was fighting to get free of the Council's grip, even as the Councilmen, too, chanted "Praise you Maiden!"

For a moment, Verna considered that maybe she had made the wrong decision. Maybe it would have been better if Verna had just let herself be the sacrifice and had let Audrey be. As far as Verna could see, nothing good would come of this.

A gust from the sea rushed in, blowing anything not pinned down across the beach, somersaulting detritus across the sand. Verna's shaggy brown hair blew back from her face as she watched the ocean seemingly part.

Up from the sunlit waves rose the bruise-colored jaws of the Elogona, its maw monstrously wide. For a moment, the boat still rocked listlessly on the ocean water, even as the water was within the beast's jaw, so big were the jaws as to not immediately disturb Audrey. But then the boat disappeared with the Elogona's frightening snap of the teeth, and soon Audrey and boat were both gone from sight.

"Praise you Maiden!" The crowd roared one last time, and everyone broke out into applause and hugs.

Not Verna. She stood up out of the bush and threw the hot geode across the beach until it crashed against Councilman Allen's back.

The sea witch's gift broke into innumerable pieces, all of which formed slithery green streaks of light. The light looked like the consistency of fluid, only it seemed to have its own consciousness as it traveled across the beach and wrapped around the townsfolk. They screamed as the green light flowed up and around them, very similar to the sea witch's tongue. The substance burned, leaving horrid scabs all over their bodies. One by one, they fell to the ground with oozing pockmarked scars until their flesh melted off like poisonous butter.

The man holding Lisbeth on his shoulders screamed. The light twirled around his ankles and crawled up his legs, bubbling as it burned through his flesh. Lisbeth tumbled to the ground and fell into a growing puddle of liquefied flesh and oozing green substance. She looked up and saw Verna in the bush. Her eyes locked onto Verna with stupefied hatred as the lower half of her body melted into the green slime.

Verna watched in horror as fires broke out, and from the geode's harsh contents, the singe of flesh, and black plumes of chemical smoke, Verna made a dash for one of the leftover fishing boats.

She hopped inside, checked quickly for oars, and took off.

As she looked back at the island, she saw the black smoke plumes form a cloud which rained down indistinguishable droplets—*eggs?*

One floated on the wind and almost fell into the water before Verna grabbed it in the palm of her hand. It was a translucent pearl-like sac.

Mervosa.

IV

Adrenaline kept Verna going for a time, but at a certain point, before pushing onward, she stared at the island and hesitated.

Should she go back?

She thought of her mother. Verna hadn't seen Jean on the beach with the rest of the townsfolk, but the Mervosa had warned that the power inside the geode wouldn't be able to stop once unleashed. Even if Verna's mother were back in the settlement, would the green poison find her? And Verna shuddered at the thought, but would it stop at the edge of the island, or would it continue onward in the atmosphere, seeking out new flesh to liquefy?

The sun beamed down on Verna's back and shoulders. She wished so much for a rainstorm.

Verna made up her mind to keep rowing until either Elogona took her, or dehydration claimed her. At the rate she was going, she wasn't sure which would happen first.

There had been many refugee ships over the years that had come to the island, and not many made it to the shore alive. The townsfolk could always see the ships as specks in the distance, but the ocean was so flat on a calm day that a person could see miles and miles toward the horizon without really appreciating how very far away it was.

That's why, when Verna did see a chunk of land on the horizon, she didn't allow herself to get hopeful. It was a piece of land she'd never seen from the shore. It didn't appear to be mainland, but it was also too distant to tell just yet.

Verna kept rowing. The monotonous circular motion of her arms made her back muscles and shoulders throb with pain. But there was nothing else to do. She couldn't quit, or she'd die. Verna had the sneaking suspicion that if she allowed herself to rest in the boat, that she might not wake up. The sun continued to beat down on her and sweat dripped from her hairline down her sunburnt face.

When the daytime finally gave way to dusk, the land looked much more in sight.

That's when she felt something pushing underneath her boat.

Was it Elogona? Was this Verna's time to die now? Would she be joining Audrey in the expansive beast of the ocean god?

Verna let one oar rest and took the other in hand, raising it above the boat in preparatory position. She knew it was fruitless to try to fight something so massive, but she could try.

She was surprised when she saw, glittering beneath the surface of the water, what could only be described as a very large fishtail. A glittery, gleaming, bulbous fishtail with a luminescent split fin at the end. The water bubbled and then a woman popped up, her curved tail behind her. Verna couldn't believe her eyes. She thought she might be hallucinating from the heatstroke.

"You'll die if you stay out here much longer," the mermaid said, and she thrust her might behind the ship. Verna was surprised at the strength of the mermaid.

The heat hit her all at once, and even though she fought it, she slid into the shell of the boat, her arm thrust over her eyes to shield the sun. She let the mermaid do the work. Verna was sure she was dreaming or hallucinating. She might not wake up, but the call of the slumber was too strong. Verna had done all she could. There was nothing to live for anymore, besides. Audrey was gone. Her parents were gone. The island was gone.

Everything left was ash and ruin. Except...

Verna eyed the pearl-like sac that had fallen into the boat, and cupped a hand gently over it to shield it from the sun's glares before she drifted into what she thought would be her final sleep.

When Verna awoke, she was surrounded by women, many of whom she had known and taken for dead. She was laid out on a boulder, her wet clothes removed, a serpentskin draped over her naked body. Verna touched her finger to it—it was papery and silky. A strange texture.

The woman applying a damp sponge to Verna's forehead was Mira. Only it couldn't be Mira because Mira had been fed to Elogona years ago. And then there was Nikki, and Jenna, and Ruth... Ruth! There were a few women Verna didn't recognize, but all around her, she saw the maidens from the past feasts, and they were alive and vibrant.

"She's awake," Mira called out, but Verna at first couldn't see who Mira was speaking to.

And then, walking through a veil of stringed shells appeared Audrey. Her blonde hair looked washed and combed, with its same upward turn at the ends. She wore an oyster-shell decoration around her breasts, and her long midsection sloped to an iridescent fishtail. Her arms were muscular—much stronger than Verna remembered, and she wondered how all of this could be possible. Audrey shimmied in a slick, fluid motion and her tail morphed back into two human legs.

"Audrey!"

Audrey stepped over to Verna's bedside, and took the sponge from Mira's hand. She rested the wet porous material against Verna's sunburnt face with tenderness.

"I'm so glad to see you," Audrey said.

"But Elogona ate you."

"It didn't eat me, silly," Audrey said. "It transformed me. It transformed all of us."

"And what's that?" Mira asked, pointing to the pearlescent egg that Verna held in her hand.

"I'm not certain, but I think it's a sea witch."

"Oh a sea witch!" A sunbathing mermaid from the

back turned her head to look. "They like shade in that stage of life. You should give it shade."

"Not like us," Mira said.

"Not like us," Audrey giggled, and her oyster-shell-decorated breasts danced as she laughed. The shells made a percussive music every time Audrey moved.

"I don't understand," Verna said.

"The Elogona swallowed me, but it couldn't digest me. There's a whole world in its belly. It changed me, Verna. I hope you don't mind."

Verna pulled Audrey in close, and smelled the scent of saltwater in her blonde hair. Verna craned her head up to kiss Audrey, and it felt like everything she'd ever wanted was finally in her grasp. Verna's body shook and she couldn't tell if it was from nerves or the sunstroke, but she let herself succumb to Audrey's embrace. Audrey held Verna in her arms, and her tongue opened Verna's lips until their tongues were twirling around each other, their bodies getting closer and closer...

... but Verna couldn't breathe.

She pushed Audrey away and hacked until her ribs hurt. Saltwater spilled out of her lungs onto the bed. She looked up to try to see Audrey but instead only saw bright, stale light...

Verna awoke, choking on saltwater. Her boat had crashed against a rocky outcrop, and she'd fallen out onto the shore.

She looked up, expecting to see Audrey or Mira, but there was no one.

It had been a dream.

A silly dream.

She crawled using her elbows to a nearby tree, to get out from under the deadly sun. The Elogona blew a mournful tune out of its organ pipes, and Verna was too dehydrated to cry, though she very much wanted to.

All Verna had wanted was lost.

She was alone.

The sight of the pearl-like sac on the sand by the boat caught Verna's eye.

Not *exactly* alone.

Verna remembered the words of Mira in her dream, and she crawled back into the sun to save the egg. It was all she had left. Egg nestled in the palm of her hand, she took it back to the shade with her.

Ash rained down on Verna as thunder clouds rolled in.

When the rain finally came, Verna got up on all fours to make a shield for the egg. There was nothing left for Verna now.

She would tend to the sea witch for the rest of her days.

Across the ocean, in the cave on the northernmost side of the island, Mervosa sat on a mountain of jittery, gel-like globules which undulated all around its gloomy antechamber. The smell of rotted flesh carried on the wind in thick drifts of black smoke, even though the Green Flame had stopped its work hours ago.

The tender-hearted were always so easy to manipulate, the sea witch thought to itself with sinister satisfaction. Eat or be eaten. That was the way.

And Mervosa liked to eat.

ACKNOWLEDGMENTS

Thank you very much to Sam, the editor and owner of Weirdpunk Books, for publishing *Elogona*. It has been a pleasure working with Weirdpunk to bring this book to readers.

My deepest appreciation goes out to the artist Evangeline Gallagher for creating the cover art. I feel honored to have such a talented artist's work accompany *Elogona*.

Additional thanks and acknowledgments go out to my dear friends: Michael Lombardo, also known as "Mike" Lombardo, Lex Quinn, Nathan Ludwig, Dino, and Waylon Jordan.

ABOUT THE AUTHOR

Samantha Kolesnik is an American fiction author, filmmaker, and film festival programmer.

She is most known for her two novellas, *True Crime* (2020) and *Waif* (2021), which were originally published by Grindhouse Press. A second edition of *Waif* is out now from Off Limits Press. She also has several works of published short fiction, including a chapbook from Tales From Between called *Lonesome Haunts*.

Her anthology *Worst Laid Plans* (now out of print), originally published by Grindhouse Press, was nominated for a Bram Stoker Award, and is now a feature film from GenreBlast Films.

Elogona is her fourth novella.

Feral Architecture: Ballardian Horrors - edited by Sam Richard

J.G. Ballard has held a tremendous influence on culture since he first started writing fiction, much of which turned out to be prophetic. In *Feral Architecture* Joe Koch, Brendan Vidito, Donyae Coles, Sara Century, and Sam Richard plume the depth of that influence on their own work through the frame of horror. The results are surreal, ominous, unexpected, unnerving, and a fitting tribute to the legacy of one of the 20th century's most impactful writers.

Chaindevils - Matthew Mitchell

Embrace the chaos with Matthew Mitchell's debut novella, which tears off pieces of horror, grimdark fantasy, dying earth fiction, and drug literature, and smashes them together in hazy, mud-coated ways unlike anything you've ever seen.

"Mitchell pens a wild extrapolation of a post-apocalyptic North American Landscape by way of *The Road*, *Warhammer 40k*, and pulp westerns. *Chaindevils* is hard, grisly fare."

Laird Barron (*The Wind Began to Howl*)

Mutant Circuit - Mark Jaskowski

What is happening to Katherine?

Someone put something into her at the plasma center and took it back out again. By the time her friends catch up to her, she's not exactly the person they remember. She has begun to change into something new, and if they're going to help her escape the people who did this to her, they may need to transform, too.

Squarely in both the crime and body horror traditions, Mutant Circuit reads like Elmore Leonard and David Cronenberg meeting at 3 AM in a run-down strip-mall parking lot, and Mark Jaskowski is the conspirator who brought them there.

"Jaskowski wields words like weapons, his prose quick and sharp as a butterfly knife. The result: a truly original work in the corpus of body horror." – Brendan Vidito (*Pornography for the End of the World, Nightmares in Ecstasy*)

Thank you for picking up this Weirdpunk book!
*We're a small press out of Minneapolis, MN and our goal
is to publish interesting and unique titles in all varieties of
weird horror and splatterpunk, often from queer writers
(though not exclusively). It is our hope that if you like one
of our releases, you will like the others.*
*If you enjoyed this book, please check out what else we
have to offer, drop a review, and tell your friends about us.
Buying directly from us is the best way to support what
we do.*
www.weirdpunkbooks.com

Printed in Great Britain
by Amazon

38176487R00081